CHILD OF THE MAY

YEARLING BOOKS are designed especially to entertain and enlighten young people. Patricia Reilly Giff, consultant to this series, received her bachelor's degree from Marymount College and a master's degree in history from St. John's University. She holds a Professional Diploma in Reading and a Doctorate of Humane Letters from Hofstra University. She was a teacher and reading consultant for many years, and is the author of numerous books for young readers.

CHILD OF THE MAY

Theresa Tomlinson

A YEARLING BOOK

Published by
Dell Yearling
an imprint of
Random House Children's Books
a division of Random House, Inc.
1540 Broadway
New York, New York 10036

Visit us on the Web! www.randomhouse.com/kids

Educators and librarians, for a variety of teaching tools, visit us at www.randomhouse.com/teachers

ISBN: 0-440-41577-2

Reprinted by arrangement with Orchard Books

Printed in the United States of America

March 2000

10 9 8 7 6 5 4 3 2 1

OPM

CONTENTS

CHILD OF THE MAY

PROLOGUE

IT WAS AUTUMN. The paths were slushy with mud and falling leaves. Two young men traveled steadily through the russet and golden woodland of Barnsdale, their faces grim.

The smaller man walked beside the horse. His scarred face was pale with silent anger that burned within, yet he led his friend's steed with great care. The taller lad, a giant of a man, hunched forward in the saddle as though he suffered from a deep hurt. In his arms he cradled a baby girl.

They slowed almost to stopping as they approached the clearing of the Forestwife. A young woman in a green kirtle chopped wood vigorously in front of a spreading thatched cottage. Though her clothes were worn and patched, about her waist she wore a beautiful woven girdle fastened with a strong metal clasp. Goats and chickens ignored the regular thumping of her ax in their hunt for food, while three cats dozed in patches of sharp sunlight. A tall boy stacked the wood carefully into a bell shape, ready for the slow burning that would turn it into charcoal. He was strongly built but, since the day he'd been caught in a mantrap, he dragged his left leg awkwardly. Suddenly the woman threw down the heavy ax and stretched her back.

"That's enough, Tom," she cried. "I'm fair worn out."

"Aye," he was quick to agree. "Shall I fetch ale?"

Before she could answer, the woman saw the silent horseman and his companion. They'd entered the clearing without a sound. She snatched up her ax again, gripping it tightly with both hands, ready to defend herself. The visitors stood beneath a great oak, still as statues. Then, suddenly, her face softened.

"Robert?" she exclaimed. "And John!"

She threw down the ax and ran to them, but slowed her steps as she saw their solemn gray faces and the small, struggling burden that they bore. "What has happened? Where is Emma? What of Bishop Hugh?"

Robert stepped forward and took hold of her by the shoulders. His voice was harsh, and his head drooped with weariness. "I'm sorry, Marian. The fighting bishop is dead. Poisoned, we swear."

"But where is Emma? John . . . where is she?"

The big man still sat astride his horse, clutching the child. He looked away shamefaced, then put his head down and wept quietly into the baby's soft brown thatch of hair.

"The king's mercenaries marched into Howden Manor," said Robert. "They were there the moment the old man died. They took his house; they took his servants; they took his horses and his fighting men. We were surrounded in the great hall while we sat at our meal. We were named as wolvesheads and ordered into the dungeon. Emma could not bear it. She ran to us, the baby in her arms. A vicious fellow, one of their captains, aimed his crossbow and shot her. Shot her in the back, there in the great hall."

"No!" Marian cried.

"Aye," he said, nodding. "There was outrage in the place

even amongst the mercenaries, and our friends rushed to our aid. We got out and found horses, hoping that we'd reach you in time, but . . ." He shook his head.

"She's dead?" Marian whispered.

Robert nodded.

"Where is she?"

"Muchlyn and Stoutley follow. They carry her in a litter, but what can we do? We bring you the child!"

Marian stepped back. "I told you not to go," she shouted. "I told you, all of you! How could you be such stupid fools to think there could be pardons!"

"You were right." Robert spoke with quiet anger. "Does it give you pleasure?"

Marian shook her head, dumb with misery.

"The child?" Robert spoke more gently. "We cannot care for her. The frosts will be on us soon."

"Take her away!" Marian cried. "I do not want the child. I want Emma."

THEY STOOD beside the fresh-piled earth of Emma's grave as the sun sank and darkness fell. Still they stood there, though the evening grew cold and the stars began to show. Then the baby whimpered in the arms of her father. John shook as though waking from a dream. He started toward the cottage, but Marian followed him and reached up to touch his shoulder. He turned to her, surprised.

"For me," she said, holding out her arms. "The baby is for me. You said that I should have her."

John dropped a kiss on the small head and gave her the child without a word.

"Magda, little Magdalen," she whispered. "Let us find you some nice, warm milk."

1

THE GREEN MAN

"HELP THEM! Help them! They will burn!"

Magda was dragged from her peaceful dream. She rubbed her eyes and shuddered as she heard the cries. Eleanor, the old one, was having one of her terrible dreams again.

Magda clapped her hands over her ears, trying to shut out the fearful sounds.

"Hunger . . . bitter hunger!" The old woman's voice rose. "They bring hunger, fire, and sword to the forest."

Magda rolled over on her straw pallet and sat up. A dark shape moved across the small sleeping space, cutting out the fire's glow for a moment. Then she heard Marian's tired voice, speaking with patience.

"Wake, Mother. 'Tis but a dream. Come, Mother, wake up and take a sip of ale."

The terror subsided to gentle sobs. Magda heaved a great sigh and settled herself down once more, pity turning to irritation as Marian's murmuring voice continued, low and soothing. Why couldn't they let her get to sleep? She'd worked hard all day. They'd made her dig up the last of the grain from the keeping pit, then pound the stuff into flour. Her arms still ached from it.

Magda had lived in this small thatched cottage deep in

Barnsdale Forest for fifteen years. Why should she stay longer with these two strange women, neither of whom was her mother? It was hard, dreary work living with the Forestwife, for the poor and the sick came from all around, begging help and healing. The clearing was rarely free from suffering—and didn't they give her the vilest jobs to do, just because she was tall and strong like her father. She was sick of digging deep latrine pits; even worse was the terrible stinking job of filling them in. The cottage leaked so that heavy rain would flood them out, and each spring they struggled to patch the wattle-framed walls with mud. Magda longed to leave the wilderness of Barnsdale and see the world beyond.

Still, she thought with a faint smile, tomorrow there'd be fresh bread and the best ale and May Day dancing. They'd raised a maypole by the trysting tree, and her father and Robert would come. Maybe they'd bring Tom with them. That thought cheered her. The Forestwife's clearing would be spinning with folk, bent on welcoming the summer and having a wild time while they were about it.

She snuggled down beneath her rug. Yes, she'd stay for the May Day dancing, but then persuade her father to take her off adventuring with him. She'd leave the forest—but a small wisp of doubt seemed to drift through her mind. What if Eleanor's dream had special meaning? What had she cried out? Hunger, fire, and sword. Many believed that what the old one saw and dreamed was the truth.

Magda could not settle down to sleep again.

All three were up early and on the move. Eleanor seemed her usual calm self once more. Even before the sun was up, they heard shouts and giggles from outside; then came a knocking on the door.

"Where's the lady?"

"Is she ready?"

"Where's our May Day Queen?"

Though she was pale and tired, Marian laughed. "They must have been up all night!" she cried. She took up her faded green cloak. "I'm getting far too old for this."

"Nay." Eleanor shook her head. "You are not too old, my daughter—but I must warn you! Maybe . . . the Green Man will miss his May Day dancing."

"What do you mean?" asked Marian.

Eleanor shook her head again. "I cannot see clear."

"Are you ready?" Magda asked. "I cannot hold them back much longer. It'll soon be sunup."

Marian nodded, and Magda threw open the door.

At once the small hut swarmed with skinny, excited children, dressed in rags but with flowers in their hair. They bore thin, starlike rushlights and a beautiful wreath of hawthorn, with its creamy, pink-tipped may blossom.

"Crown the queen! Crown the queen!" they chanted. Marian bowed her head to be crowned.

The clearing was lit with flickering candles and lanterns. Marian went to stand before the maypole, while the children rushed off into the forest. The gathering turned quiet, waiting in tense silence. Magda stood beside Marian, her heart beating fast. This was the moment that she'd always loved, ever since she was a tiny child. Her hand crept into Marian's and squeezed it hard. Then they heard it, gentle at first, faint sounds of chanting.

"Summer is a-coming in! Summer is a-coming in!"

It grew steadily louder, until streams of children broke from the cover of the trees, dragging ropes of plaited ivy. They hauled their ropes as the sun came up, dragging a dark figure from the depth of the forest. It was hard to see him clearly at first, for, like the very trees, he was covered in leaves and blossoms.

Marian turned to the old one. "He comes, after all your fears."

Eleanor smiled and nodded.

At last he strode from the shade out into the growing sunlight—the frightening, wonderful, magical Green Man.

Magda stared at him. This was not Robert! Ever since she could remember, Robert had been the Green Man. He'd come each May Day to dance with the Forestwife. This man was huge, but he leapt across the clearing with the grace of a deer. His thick beard was as green as his skin. Magda's heart thumped faster than ever as he came toward them. Could this truly be the spirit of the forest, the guardian of the plants and trees?

"It's really him!" she whispered, and clutched at Marian's cloak.

A fleeting moment of disappointment touched the woman's face. Then quickly Marian smiled. She reached up to her crown of may blossom and swiftly placed it on Magda's head.

"You shall be Green Lady today," she whispered.

"Nay," Magda cried out.

"Oh yes," Marian insisted, laughing now. "Go greet the Green Man."

Magda turned fearfully toward the terrifying figure that danced toward her. Then suddenly she was laughing too and racing to him, her arms outstretched.

"My father, my father!" she shouted. "My father is the Green Man!"

2

A Place of
Ancient Magic

THE DAY WAS FILLED with wild laughter and dancing, but in the evening the clearing quieted as young men and women slipped off in pairs into the forest. As dusk fell, Marian found Magda and dragged her back into the hut.

"But I want to dance with Tom," Magda complained.

"Tom can come inside too," Marian insisted. "Your father sits by our fireside, and there's much to talk about."

"You're angry because Robert's not here," Magda snapped. "If you can't have any fun, then neither can I!"

Marian did not deny it, just shrugged her shoulders and sighed. Then Magda wished that she had kept silent as she glimpsed the shadow of sadness that crossed Marian's face. Couldn't she keep her mouth shut? Was it not hurtful enough that Robert was not there to dance with the Forestwife? Magda quietly did as she was told, contenting herself with sitting down beside Tom and leaning with pleasure against his strong back.

"Well?" Marian looked across at John as he sprawled beside the hearthstone, still wiping traces of green dye from his cheeks. "What is it now that keeps him?"

John sighed. "He travels through Sherwood into Nottingham Town."

"What? Is he gone completely mad?"

John shook his head. "Aye, maybe so! But I must follow him in the morning—and when you hear it all, you'll see that something had to be done. Your friend Philippa will go with us."

"Philippa?" cried Marian. "I was surprised that she didn't come today. Tell me quickly!"

"It was only yesterday that we discovered it," said John. "We stopped by Langden village on our way to you. Lady Matilda was worried sick, and all the villagers were rushing about the place. Matilda and her daughter, Isabel, have been summoned to Nottingham by King John."

"What? The king's in Nottingham too?"

"Aye. He celebrates May Day with the sheriff, and we've heard that he has sold the man the shrievalties of Derbyshire and Yorkshire!"

"Oh, no!" Marian gasped. "So Gilbert de Gore is sheriff of all three counties? That puts paid to Robert's trick of crossing the borders for safety."

"It does," John agreed. "We'd have far to go to be free of his bullying laws."

"I begin to worry," said Marian grimly. "What do they want with Matilda?"

John shook his head. "It seems the king wants Isabel to marry one of his men. Langden lands will be used as a reward. Isabel has made the lands rich and fertile. You could feed an army from them."

"But that's not right," Marian cried. "Matilda raised every penny she could and bought permission to marry her daughter where she wished."

"Aye," Tom butted in. "Lady Matilda stripped Langden of everything of value to pay the king's price, and we've never regretted it, for Isabel has more than repaid the villagers with her kindness."

John shrugged his shoulders. "When was anything ever fair? This king's as greedy for money as his brother was, and he's slippery as an eel. Now he says that Isabel is well past the age when she should marry, and she must marry the man of his choosing or pay the freedom tax once more."

"He can't do that!" Marian was outraged.

John laughed bitterly. "He does what he wants. Even the barons are growing to hate him. He invents his own taxes all the time. But this cruelty to Isabel will hurt all of us. Some manor lords would have bled their own peasants dry to build up their funds, but not Lady Matilda. She and Isabel have nothing but the house and the land they own."

"What will happen now?" Magda asked anxiously.

John stroked his beard thoughtfully. "The king demands that they present themselves at Nottingham Castle, so off they've gone. They cannot refuse, even though Lady Matilda's so frail."

"And so," Marian said with resignation, "Robert has gone with them?"

"Not exactly with them," said John. "There's Brother James and Much and Will Stoutley too, all going into Nottingham by their own secret ways. Philippa insists on coming as well. We shall stick close to our two Langden ladies, doing our best to keep them from harm. Now do you see why Tom and I must follow tomorrow?"

"Yes," said Marian, turning to Eleanor, who sat very still beside her, looking troubled. "Do you see aught to fear, Mother?"

"Nothing clear," she said, shivering a little. "Just cold and hunger, cold and hunger and thirst."

Marian sighed. "I am weary of this struggle," she said. "It goes on and on, and we can never win."

"We must rise early in the morning," said Tom, yawning. "We need as many pairs of ears and eyes as we can get."

"Right," said Magda. "Then I shall go too."

"You shall not," said Marian.

Magda jumped to her feet and stamped out of the hut, banging the door hard behind her. She marched off toward the edge of the stream, kicked off her boots, and slipped her feet into the water. The comforting warm spring bubbled up from deep inside the earth, soothing her a little. Hot tears of anger filled her eyes, blurring the moonlit woodland.

They treated her like a child, like a prisoner almost.

Faint rustling came to her as she looked into the darkness beyond the babbling water. Bushes twitched, and she heard the sounds of low laughter. This night was supposed to be special for young women and their sweethearts. Some couples had built bowers for their courting, filled with scented herbs and flowers. There'd be babies born from this night's loving. Was she not such a one herself? Child of the May, her father called her.

The door of the hut opened again, and she heard her father calling her name. She got up and went slowly toward him.

"Come here, Magda," he begged.

John went to sit on the doorstep, pulling Magda down beside him. He put his arms about her, hugging her tightly.

"You are the most precious thing in the world to me," he said.

Magda sighed. She loved her father dearly, but she'd heard it all before. "I know," she said. "I am all that's left to you of your beloved Emma."

"You do not know how cruel this world is!" he told her. "Here in this clearing, you are safe. There's ancient magic in the place."

"Safe! Safe!" Magda exploded. "But Father, I do not want to be safe!"

She pushed John away and strode back into the cottage. Marian looked up as the girl stormed in, angry and tear-stained.

"Don't look at me like that," Magda cried. "I will go, whatever you say. This place may be enough for you, but it is not enough for me!" She threw herself down onto her pallet, turning her face away from her friends.

"Leave her! Let her stew!" said Marian, but Eleanor went quietly to sit beside her, stroking Magda's hair in silence. Tom looked uncomfortable.

Marian stared angrily into the fire until John came back inside. "Come sit beside me, John," she said, holding out her hand to him. "You and I must take counsel over this unruly child of yours."

John and Marian whispered together late into the night, while the others slept.

3

THE YOUNG VIXEN

MAGDA WAS awakened early by the sharp bang of wood on wood. Marian had built up the fire so that it flared and crackled. A fine smell came from freshly made oatcakes sizzling on the flat iron griddle that hung over the hearthstone. Magda sat up and watched, bleary-eyed, as Marian rummaged purposefully in the wooden box that contained the few worn scraps of clothing they possessed.

Magda groaned and pushed her warm rug away, swinging her long legs to the side. "What are you doing?" she asked. "It's not even sunup! You look as though you've been awake all night."

"I have," said Marian.

Magda frowned. "Can't you let decent folk sleep?"

The older woman pulled out a worn pair of breeches that had once belonged to Tom. "These will do," she exclaimed. "And a cloak and hood. That's what's needed."

Magda got up and stretched. She stood there, hands on hips, watching with irritation. Suddenly Marian swung around and held the breeches up in front of Magda, as though measuring them against her.

"What are you doing? I'm not wearing them!"

"You are," said Marian. "You'll wear these breeches if

you're going to Nottingham with the men. And keep that sullen look upon your face—sharp as arrowheads, that look is. It will protect you well!"

Magda's mouth dropped open; her hands fell to her sides.

"Don't stand and gawp!" Marian snapped. "John and I've agreed. You can go if you dress as a lad and if you stay close to him or Philippa."

Magda was amazed. "Or Robert," she said.

"He'll get you into trouble worse than any," Marian replied sharply. Then she sighed. "Or Robert," she agreed.

"I'm going to Nottingham! I'm going to Nottingham!" Magda cried.

All at once the snappiness drained from Marian's voice. "Truth is," she said, "you are not growing up much like Emma. Last night you put me more in mind of someone else. Someone I remembered from long ago."

Magda frowned, puzzled by her words. "What do you mean?"

Marian shook her head. Then she laughed, though the sound she made was harsh. "Myself," she said. "You put me in mind of the girl that I once was. I fear it's more like me that you grow, not your gentle mother. Believe me, Magda, there are times when I wish myself far away from this place. I may not go, but you can. It seems the time has come."

Magda blinked hard. Her eyes brimmed with tears, and her heart filled up with a sudden, fierce love. She flung her arms around Marian. "I am happy if I grow like you," she said.

"Aye, well," said Marian, smiling and pushing her gently away. "Let's hope you've learned enough to keep you safe. Now there's no time for worrying; we must sort things out. There's much to do."

"Must I really wear Tom's old breeches?" Magda sniffed at them suspiciously.

Marian nodded firmly. She pulled out the sharp meat knife that she always carried tucked into her girdle.

"You must wear breeches, cloak, and hood, and that shiny chestnut mane must go. A tall, handsome lass like you with all that lovely hair will cause a stir. Your father has trouble enough keeping himself from being noticed."

"Aye," Magda agreed. "Not like Robert."

Marian smiled wryly. Robert came and went mysteriously, like a flying shadow. He robbed rich bishops in Yorkshire one day and fooled the sheriff's guard in Nottingham the next. The Hooded One was what they called him, and ridiculous stories of his doings had spread throughout the north of England. Rich rewards had been offered for his capture, alive or dead. Certainly he had become the most wanted man in the north.

"Aye," said Marian sadly. "He keeps his secrets, does Robert."

The sharp blade swished, and dark chestnut locks fell all about Magda's feet like autumn leaves.

At last Marian stood back. "It's done," she said.

Magda brushed the itchy coating of cut hairs from around her neck and tossed her head from side to side. "Feels funny," she muttered.

"Does it feel bad?"

"Nay," said Magda, flicking her hands through the short strands that now swung neatly just beneath her ears. "Nay, it feels fine. It feels free."

"Good," said Marian, smiling with relief. "Now take up these oatcakes and carry them round to your father. See if he knows you!"

When the girl had gone, Marian's smile faded. Wearily she gathered up the dark locks of hair, stuffing them into a basket. But when the job was done and the basket set aside, she turned impulsively back to it and snatched up a small handful of the soft curls. She went to the salt crock and took up a pinch of the precious stuff, then sprinkled hair and salt together in a circle above the fire. The hair and salt flared with a swift blue flame. Marian spat into the fire, and as it hissed she murmured,

> *"Water, earth, air, and fire bright,*
> *Keep my girl safe, both day and night."*

THEY LEFT soon after sunrise. Magda strode ahead, delighting in the new freedom that Tom's breeches brought. She was filled with excitement and energy for the coming journey. John and Tom followed more slowly, with many a backward glance at the small figure of Marian. She stood by the ancient turning stone that marked the entrance to the Forestwife's clearing, watching till they had vanished from sight.

They went to the south and reached Langden village when the sun was high in the sky. Magda thought that Langden seemed unusually quiet.

The villagers' small cots were built close to the main cart track. The manor house stood proud on a mound with a deep ditch all around. It was well cared for and surrounded by orchards, pigs and good-sized vegetable strips all fenced in with low palings. At times the villagers complained that the manor had no defenses, but Isabel insisted that she was a farmer, not a fighter. She ignored the villagers' fears and fed them well.

Philippa was waiting by the forge in her best gown and cloak, with her husband the blacksmith. She kissed Tom and tugged at his beard.

"You are more of a man than ever," she said. Though Tom was twenty-six and a tall, good-looking man, Philippa had known him since he was a baby and still thought of him that way. "When are you coming back to Langden? We miss you here—this was once your home!"

Tom shook his head. "I can't come back," he said. "Not since Mam died."

Philippa nodded her understanding. "But who's this young lad?" she asked, glancing at Magda and winking at John.

"A lad I'd rather see safe at home," John told her. "But he's promised to stay close by us, has this lad."

"Right enough," Philippa agreed. "The time comes for each young vixen to creep from her den."

"Aye," said John. "She may creep from her den, but can she hunt?"

Philippa hugged her husband and Rowan, her youngest son, a fair-haired lad two years older than Magda.

"I think I should be going with you," said Rowan teasingly. "If Magda's going, so should I."

Philippa gave him a playful punch on the cheek. "You've to stay here and take care of our guest from Mansfield," she told him, glancing back to where a man stood half hidden in the dark entrance to the forge.

Magda looked at him and gasped. Just for one moment she thought that it was Robert. Was that not Robert's cloak and hood? She knew it well. Then he moved forward into the light, and she saw that his face was strange to her. The man glared angrily at them, then turned back to the warm fire inside the forge.

"Who is he?" Magda asked.

Philippa snorted with raucous laughter and took Magda by the arm. "He's a guest," she said. "Unwilling, but still a guest. Come, let's get on our way at once, for we must reach Sherwood before nightfall. Langden shall see no peace or thriving until Matilda and Isabel have returned."

4

THE WOLF PACK

THE WASTES AND WOODLANDS were lush with springing grass and bursting yellow-green buds; the undergrowth was alive with young hares and waddling partridges. The scent of sap and blossom hung in the air.

"Maytime! Maytime! Best time of all the year!" Magda cried.

"Not bad," Philippa admitted. "A good dry time for taking to the road. At least we shan't be shivering in a ditch tonight."

"I wish your Rowan could have come." Magda sighed, seeing again his handsome face and teasing smile.

"Eh, lass! Isn't one strong lad enough company for you?" Philippa lowered her voice, nodding behind them at Tom.

"Huh! Tom's fine and I love him," said Magda. "But he does drag his leg so. Besides, he's more of a brother to me."

"You weren't there when Tom near snapped that leg in a mantrap," said Philippa darkly. "I was. I tell you this for nothing: though Rowan is the apple of my eye, you'll never find a braver lad than Tom—not in the whole of Yorkshire."

"Well," said Magda cheekily, "aren't we in Notting-hamshire now?"

She ducked fast as Philippa's hand swung close to her cheek.

They reached the edge of Sherwood as the sun began to sink. Tom led them through secret paths to a small cave mouth.

"They were here," he said, dropping to his knees to sniff at a light patch of wood ash that lay within a darkened circle of burned earth. "Yes, Robert and Much. Two days ahead."

Magda stared at him. "Daft lad," she muttered.

"If Tom tells you so, you'd best believe it," John told her.

"How?" Magda still doubted.

"A faint smell of burning." Tom held a pinch of ash to her nose. "That will be gone by sunrise; and see how it's raked out in a circle with one stone dropped into the center here—that's Robert. And the small white pebble—that's Much. The circle is broken here; they've traveled on to the south."

"Huh," said Magda. "And I suppose you'll be telling me what they ate for their supper?"

"Venison," said Tom. "Smoked venison."

"How can you tell that?"

Tom gave a wicked laugh. "Because I smoked the meat for him myself and wrapped it up in burdock leaves. Anyway, it's what the Hooded One always eats when he's journeying and there's no time to make a fresh kill."

They quickly got a fire kindled and settled to eat Marian's bread and goat cheese.

"I thought you'd snare us a hare or shoot a fat partridge," said Magda, disappointed.

"Nay," said John. "We must leave them to raise their young in spring, then we shall eat well of them when winter comes. Besides, who'd want burned meat when they can have fresh bread?"

They slept in the sheltering cave, wrapped in their cloaks, with sweet-smelling rushes piled beneath them. In the morning they woke with the sun and ate the rest of their food. They were on the road to Nottingham by the time the sun was above the trees.

As the great city rose in the distance before them, the road became thronged with rumbling carts, packhorses, and dust-stained travelers heading for the main northern gate.

Magda grabbed Philippa by the arm. "Look there!" she yelled, her cheeks pink with the excitement of it all. "See the towers that soar high into the sky? Is that Nottingham Castle? How does it float up there above us? But look . . . in that fine wagon. A lady dressed in scarlet with gold on her head! Is she the queen? She must be the queen!"

Philippa could only laugh. She turned to John. "Look at this lad of yours. His eyes are fair popping at the sights."

John could not smile. He put his hand on Magda's shoulder. "Look and stare as much as you wish, but stay close, I beg."

"Don't fret so." Magda waggled her shoulders impatiently, moving away from his protective touch.

A horn sounded three times behind them. "Wolf pack! Wolf pack!" The cry rose all about.

There came the sound of galloping hooves, and panic spread as folk dragged their wagons and mules to the side of the road. Philippa grabbed Magda and pulled her through the scrambling crowd. The horses were moving fast. Stragglers threw themselves into the ditches as a large party of armed soldiers galloped by on huge, snorting horses. They sped along the road, regardless of people still struggling to get out of their way. There were cries and screams, and everyone was spattered with mud and filth.

"Christ have mercy!" shrieked a woman who landed almost on top of Magda, leaping into the ditch just as the soldiers passed. "They've crushed my toe!" she yelled.

Magda rolled over and turned to her with concern. "Let me see." She was used to treating crushed toes and feet.

The woman ignored the young person trying to help her and continued to yell after the gang of soldiers fast disappearing into the distance in a cloud of dust. She screamed and held up two fingers. "Hell and damnation take them!" she cried. "The Witch of Barnsdale curse them!"

"Witch of Barnsdale?" said Magda, puzzled, carefully taking the woman's foot into her hands to massage the toes.

"Aye," said the woman, turning to her at last. "You must have heard of her, lad—the evil Witch of Barnsdale? The one they call the Forestwife? They say she's enchanted the Hooded One and keeps him from the gallows with her spells!"

"Why, of course!" said Philippa hastily. "Of course he's heard such tales, but I daresay they're all rubbish."

"Oh . . . yes!" said Magda quickly.

Now the woman was staring down at her foot as Magda worked her fingers gently up and down. "Why, that feels better, lad!" she cried, soldiers and witches all forgotten. "Good as new! I thought they'd crippled me. Thank you— you're an angel sent from heaven. Where did you learn to do that?"

Philippa took hold of Magda by the arm, hurrying her away to where John and Tom waited anxiously. "He's a grand lad," she called back, "but we must be getting on or we'll be late."

The woman stared after them. "Bless you both!" she cried.

"Walk on; walk fast!" Philippa muttered. "Try not to cause a stir."

Magda obeyed, but as soon as they were on their way, she had to satisfy her curiosity. "Evil Witch of Barnsdale?" she spluttered. "And who were those men? The ones they called the wolf pack?"

"The king's special guard," John told her through gritted teeth. "Mercenaries every one; more feared than any. They're no dutiful feudal gathering, but trained fighters who kill for money. They'll do any filthy deed the king wishes so long as he pays enough."

Magda shivered and moved closer to her father.

THE POTTER OF
MANSFIELD

IT WAS AFTER NOON when they passed over the deep ditch and in through the northern gate of Nottingham Town. They walked across the marketplace. The market was in full swing, rowdy with the shouts of peddlers and stallholders, but above all the bustle loomed the great stone towers of the castle, built upon a high rock.

Magda was distracted by the market sights and sounds, her head muddled with the clamor and her nose twitching at the strange mixture of smells.

"Spices from Araby! Cinnamon and ginger!" A woman wafted a pinch of sharp-smelling brown powder beneath her nose.

"Fresh pies!" another shouted.

"Sweet honey cakes!"

"Fine roast pork! Fill your belly! Salted crackling!"

Philippa grabbed Magda's arm and led her boldly on toward the castle.

"Not here," she insisted. "Look out for a potter's stall."

Magda wondered what on earth they could want with pots when Lady Matilda and Isabel were in danger, but she was so amazed by all that she saw that she didn't argue. John and Tom followed as she and Philippa went on through the stone-built gateway and into the castle's outer bailey. Here there were more stalls and bustle, but Philippa took a quick look around and marched on over the next bridge and into the middle bailey.

"There." Tom spoke quietly. "I see him."

John swore under his breath. "Damn the man. Can he get no closer? Must he sit under the sheriff's nose? Next he'll be in the sheriff's kitchens."

Philippa shrugged her shoulders. "Best place to see what's going on."

The middle bailey was alive with soldiers and horses and kitchen maids buying produce from stalls and peddlers. Magda looked about for Robert, but she could see no sign of him. There were just two pottery stalls and a loudmouthed fellow in a straw hat grabbing all the customers with his shouting of wares and low prices. Then all at once she saw Brother James, handing out benedictions to the castle guards and collecting pennies in a bowl, a saintly look upon his face. John went to him and knelt down.

Brother James made the sign of the cross and whispered in his ear. John answered, and Brother James looked piously up to heaven and spoke again, as though chanting.

"A long blessing this is going to be!" Philippa folded her arms and tapped her foot.

When at last John returned, they clustered about him.

"Well?"

"What's up?"

John sighed and wouldn't be rushed. "Robert's worried about Isabel. King John has told Matilda that she must pay him four hundred pounds or marry her daughter to some murderous soldier captain. Robert and Brother James want us to find a horse and have it ready up by the northern gate.

They've seen that the wolf pack has arrived. Brother James has his eye on their steeds—trust him."

"Nay!" Philippa swore quietly. "Does he think we're tired of living?"

"Just one," said John. "One good, fast horse to hitch to the wagon. Lady Matilda cannot ride."

"We could maybe manage to steal just one of their mounts," said Tom. "There's plenty of us to distract them while it's taken."

"Not Magda," said John. "I'll not have my lass at risk. This is what I feared."

"Leave her with Robert," said Philippa. "He's only watching, isn't he?"

John looked anxious. "When did he ever just watch?"

Magda stared about her, puzzled. "Robert? He's not even here."

Her friends laughed quietly, and John relented. He put his arm around his daughter's shoulder and gently turned her toward the noisy potter's stall. "Our Robert is here all right, my darling. Go up to yon fellow with the plates. Stand behind the table as though you were the potter's lad and do not move from the man's side."

Magda took a few hesitant steps toward the busy stall and then stopped. There, chalked at the top of the wooden frame for all to see, was a circle with one white shape in the middle.

"Ah!" She caught her breath. "Robert's sign!" She turned quickly then to look at the man who stood shouting and bawling in the center of the crowd. His face was turned away from her, and she could not see him clearly as the crowds pressed so close.

"Best Mansfield earthenware!" he sang out. "Goodwives,

you'll never find better! Plates and bowls, fine enough for the sheriff's own table!"

Magda stared at the back of the potter's neck. How could it be him? This was not Robert's quiet, angry way of speaking. The hat he wore was covered with fine spatters of dried clay. Magda moved closer. Even the hair at the back of his neck was clay-streaked. Then he turned, and she saw at once the ugly scar that marred his cheek. It was Robert. Ever since she'd been tiny she'd shuddered at the sight of that scar. But where had all these pots come from? All at once she understood; she remembered the angry face of the man who sheltered in Langden forge. An unwilling guest from Mansfield, Philippa had said.

Suddenly Magda's stomach lurched, for Robert had seen her. He looked directly at her through the shoving crowd. Would he know her, disguised like this? Just for one brief moment he frowned and hesitated, but then quickly he shouted at her.

"So there you are, you rascal! Where have you been? Pass me those platters! I can't keep pace, they're so greedy for pots in Nottingham today!"

Magda blinked and swallowed hard, then dived behind the stall to do as he asked. As soon as she had time to pause, she glanced back at her father. Tom and Philippa strode off toward the castle stables. John followed them slowly.

The potter of Mansfield and his lad worked hard. Never at any time did Robert speak to her as anything other than his apprentice, but at one point when she turned to pick up a fine set of platters from the back of the stall, he told her to let them be.

"Not those," he hissed. "I'm hoping that I'll get a special

customer for those, what with the wolf pack arriving unexpectedly and the castle full of guests."

Magda did not understand what he meant, but she was distracted by the loud complaints that came from the man in the next stall.

"No profit at those prices," he grumbled to his boy. "Might as well pack up—the light is fading fast. Set about it, and don't you drop aught this time."

The other potter's lad looked utterly miserable. Magda could not help but feel a touch sorry and bent close to whisper in his ear. "We'll not be here next week."

The boy glowered and showed her his fist, and Magda remembered that he must suppose her to be a lad.

She had a job not to giggle, but stood back and tried again in a deep, gruff voice. "My master may be selling plates cheaply today," she said, "but he'll be off to another town next week. Then your master will have his custom back."

The boy scowled. "Mind your own business," he said, making fists of both his hands and throwing a punch close to Magda's face. "Watch out!" he warned her. "I'm training to be a squire." He pulled a cheaply made dagger from his belt and swung it close to her cheek.

Magda was not John's daughter for nothing. She made a tight fist and hit him smartly on the chin. The lad went down, sprawling at her feet, the dagger clattering onto the cobbles. His jerkin slipped open, revealing a strange red patch beneath his collarbone.

Magda stared, and the lad covered himself quickly.

"Does that pain you?" Magda asked. She felt a twinge of grudging respect for the lad's fearless assault on someone so much taller.

"Nay." The boy spoke sharply. "Not at all."

Magda took the boy's hand and pulled him to his feet. "You're hot," she said. "Feverish?"

"No," he insisted, sticking the dagger back into his belt.

So many years spent in the Forestwife's clearing brought Marian's wisdom flooding into Magda's head. "Have you tried a lavender brew?"

"To drink?" The boy's eyes showed reluctant interest.

"Nay. Brew it up, then let it cool and dab it on that sore patch."

All at once the boy's hands were shaking. He pulled two pennies from his pouch and without another word was off, running between the stalls to where the herbwives sold their wares.

Magda turned back to the Mansfield potter's stall, a little shaken. Truth was, she'd never seen a sore quite like that strange patch.

"Shall we pack up?" she asked Robert. "You've nothing left to sell—only your special platters. Everyone else is going."

"Hush!" Robert smiled as a sudden flurry of noise and movement started up in the entrance to the castle kitchens. "I believe my special customer arrives."

6

THE SHERIFF'S WIFE

AN ANGRY MAID and a young kitchen lad ran out of the castle. Their aprons were smeared with fat and flour, their sleeves rolled up, their faces pink and sweating.

"See! It's too late, they're all going," the maid cried.

"Nay, here's one." The lad caught her arm and pointed to the Mansfield potter's stall. "And look—a pile of decent platters left. Will you wait a moment, good potter?"

"I'll go and fetch my lady," said the maid.

Magda felt her heart thudding fast. Whatever was Robert up to now?

" 'Tis like hell in that kitchen," the lad complained. "You'd think we'd got enough to do finding food and drink for the king and his court, without the wolf pack arriving as well! Drink like fishes they do, and now we've run out of platters." The lad made a fearful face and crossed himself. "Sheriff's lady is right put out! She don't like to spend her pennies needlessly."

Robert shook his head wisely. "Doesn't do to offend those fellows."

"You're right," the lad answered with feeling.

"Don't fret," said Robert. "The potter of Mansfield shall come to your mistress's aid."

The maid appeared again, with an older woman whose silver ladle thrust through her belt marked her as cook. A young page in smart velvet livery burst from the kitchen behind them, and after him followed the grandest woman that Magda had ever set eyes on.

The sheriff's lady was plump and at least fifty. She was dressed in crimson velvet with gold trimmings. The high waist of her gown unfortunately made her large stomach appear even rounder. A headdress wreathed in veils had slipped slightly to the side, giving her the look of a disgruntled cow. Her fingers were covered in rings, her long nails rouged. Just like her servants, she was pink and sweating, and she rubbed her jeweled hands together anxiously.

"You'd better be right," she snapped at the cook. "Have you got my purse?" She slapped the small page on the head.

"Yes, madam," he squeaked, holding up a leathern drawstring pouch.

"Fancy having to buy earthenware," she muttered.

"Better than no platters at all," the cook told her firmly.

By now she was standing before the stall, and Robert bowed low to her. Magda almost curtsied, but remembered in time and copied his deep bow.

"I hear my lady is short of platters for her guests," Robert said. With one swift movement he gathered up the pile of good earthenware that he'd saved and spread it across the stall.

"Hmm! Not bad!" the woman cried. "Though I daresay this will cost me a pretty penny."

"Ah, no, lady." Robert spoke quickly. A certain flinty glance at Magda warned her to say nothing, whatever came next. He gave a great sigh and smiled boldly at the sheriff's wife. "For such a lovely lady, the price is . . . nothing at all.

It is an honor to serve such beauty. A gift from the potter of Mansfield."

All the servants gaped, and Magda had great trouble keeping still and quiet, but the sheriff's wife went pinker still and giggled. She flapped her bejeweled hand at Robert.

"Why, Sir Potter," she said, "I fear you are a very wicked fellow. I accept your gift, and . . . you shall dine with us tonight."

"Ah, no!" Robert was all modesty and hesitation.

"Yes, you shall—you and your lad! Come, pack up your stall and fetch in these platters. I shall make space for you among my guests." And with those words she swept away, leaving her servants openmouthed.

Robert was not for wasting time; he clapped his hands, smiling wickedly at Magda. "Come on, boy! We're dining at the castle."

THE KITCHEN lad had spoken truly, for the castle kitchens were indeed like hell. Cauldrons bubbled over fires, suspended from great chains hooked on to wooden beams. Huge spitted roasts of meat flamed and spluttered in the hearths. The place was crammed with servants, squabbling and shouting and getting in one another's way. Torches were fixed to brackets on the walls, but they gave off little light and a lot of smoke. A young servant girl heaved a steaming bucket of water past Magda, slopping it on her arm and making her gasp.

"Sorry, sir," the servant cried. "But it's no good you standing there—I shall be back for another in a moment. 'Tis for the king's bathtub. Terrible clean and fussy, he is. Says he must bathe before he eats. Have you ever heard of such a thing?"

"Come," said Robert, taking hold of Magda's arm. "Come stand at the end of the great hall and see if our grand lady remembers to give us a place."

He led Magda through the madness of the kitchens and up the steps into the enormous hall. Already people were gathering for the evening meal. Set upon a raised platform at the far end, the high table was empty. Six long trestle tables laid out in rows were filling up with soldiers, ladies-in-waiting, and guests of lesser importance.

"Where shall we sit?" Magda asked, half fascinated, half alarmed by the excitement of it all.

"Just stand and watch," said Robert. "That suits me well for the moment. Ah, yes . . . as I hoped."

Magda followed his gaze and saw a young woman in a homespun gown leading a frail old lady. Isabel and Matilda, their poverty more apparent than ever in such gaudy surroundings.

"Watch them closely," said Robert. "Ah, I see that help arrives."

Magda could not stop herself from smiling at the sight of Brother James slowly parading up and down the hall, still handing out blessings in a most condescending manner.

"Who could have invited him?" she wondered.

Robert snorted and grimaced. "Nobody," he said. "Priest's garb and knowledge of the Mass will take the man anywhere."

"Where is Much?" Magda asked.

"Guarding the potter's wagon, up by the northern gate, I hope."

Trumpets sounded, and everyone rushed to take their seats at the trestle tables. Robert pushed Magda toward the long bench set opposite Langden's ladies. There was a scramble to sit down, and for a moment Magda and Isabel looked straight at each other. Just the slight raising of an eyebrow told them that Isabel recognized her fellow guests. The trumpet sounded again, and everyone struggled to their feet as the king and his queen arrived and took their seats. The sheriff and his wife bowed and curtsied profusely, fussing nervously as King John sat down.

Magda strained her neck to stare at the man whose cruelty was feared throughout the land.

"He's thin and small," she whispered. "And look at the queen. She's nowt but a lass!"

Before Robert could reply, Magda felt a heavy hand upon her shoulder.

"Out of my way, lad. How dare you sit across from my lady!"

Magda yelped as she was cuffed over the ear and thrust aside. A powerfully built, heavy-jowled man with a close-shaved chin bent across the table and snatched up Isabel's reluctant hand to kiss.

"Get out," Robert whispered, pulling Magda along behind him toward the end of the next table, where Brother James sat.

"He hit me!" Magda cried, red-faced and rubbing her hurt. "Aren't you going to stand up for me?"

Robert's face had gone white. His voice hissed with anger as he spoke. "I promise you this, my child: death shall be too good for that one. But now is not the time."

"Who is he?" Magda demanded.

"Hugh FitzRanulf," he told her. "Leader of the wolf pack. Dealer in misery!"

7

To Dine with the Sheriff's Wife

BROTHER JAMES quickly made room for them on the bench beside him, and the meal began. Though the table was groaning with food, Magda could not eat. Her head thudded and her stomach heaved. Excitement had turned to fear.

"Can we not slip away now?" she whispered, suddenly longing for the wildness and safety of the Forestwife's clearing.

Brother James seemed to be calmly eating up everything within reach, but Robert spoke low and answered her. "We've not done what we came for yet. You'd do best to eat. Who knows when we'll eat again! Here, share my trencher and cup."

Reluctantly seeing the sense in his words, Magda took a sip of heady spiced wine and began picking at a leg of roast chicken. She tried not to look at Robert's scarred cheek and slit ear. In the rush to find a seat, she'd sat down on his right-hand side, something she usually avoided. The meal continued, and the servants were in and out of the kitchen, bringing platters piled high with roast swan and heron. Gentle strumming of harps from the musicians up in the gallery soothed her a little, as did the sweet scent of violets and green herbs strewn on the floor. Her spirits lifted at the sight of an array of delicious desserts.

Though Robert had told her to eat, he seemed distracted and ate little himself. Magda sensed a tension in the man. He looked up toward the top table and silently reached out to touch Brother James. Although the fat monk did not move a muscle, Magda saw that he was instantly alert, all pleasure in food forgotten.

"A messenger!" Robert told him. "Could it be they have discovered John and the stolen horse?"

Suddenly the king was on his feet and flinging his wine cup across the table so that the strong red liquid splashed across the fine gowns of the ladies-in-waiting.

"Matilda! Damn the woman!" he screamed. "I'll have her now!"

Magda gasped, but Robert pressed her arm. "Hush," he whispered. "Not our Matilda, surely."

"FitzRanulf!" the king shouted. "Leave your food, man! Get your fellows up to the Scottish border. I have her at last—the lady de Braose."

"See," Robert soothed. "Not our lady. It's Matilda de Braose, wife to William. Powerful border lord, he is—or was."

"Brave woman," growled Brother James. "I sorrow to hear her captured. His wolves have chased her through half the kingdom!"

There was no time for Magda to ask more; the great hall was in an uproar. The wolf pack rose quickly from their seats at the king's command. Wine spilled; kitchen lads and lasses were shoved aside; bread and meat rolled to the floor.

"Look sharp," hissed Robert. "This may be our moment. Make for Isabel."

Caught in the chaos, Isabel looked wildly about her, sure that she'd had a glimpse of Brother James. "Thank God!"

she cried at the sight of him battling sturdily through the crowd toward her, two familiar figures behind him.

"Come, dear lady," Brother James said, gently lifting Matilda of Langden into his arms. "We think it time to go."

Robert took Isabel's arm and steered her toward the kitchens. "Let's leave," he whispered. "None will think of you at this moment."

Magda followed them as best she could, but Robert had been wrong. The sheriff's wife stood just inside the kitchen, marshaling her servants to save what food they could.

"I want no waste!" she shrieked, her face red and sweaty. "And where do you go, my lady of Langden?" she demanded.

For just one terrible moment Robert seemed to hesitate. Magda shivered, despite the heat and fuss that surrounded them.

"Why, to their home, fair lady." Robert was quickly silken-tongued and confident again. "The potter of Mansfield shall see them safely to Langden."

"Oh, would you indeed, Sir Potter?" The sheriff's wife twitched with surprise at such boldness. "But you would pass through Sherwood and Barnsdale! How can you and your young lad protect these ladies from murderous thieves?"

"Ah, we can outwit the Hooded One." Robert winked. "We potters have our own safe and secret byways. Besides, 'twill save you the expense of keeping these ladies here."

The woman still doubted. "Isabel?" she said. "Would you go off with these men? You were told to marry or pay the fine."

"I cannot think of marriage when my mother is sick," Isabel answered firmly. "She craves the comfort of her own hearth. I know this man and I trust him."

The sheriff's wife folded her arms and pursed her lips.

Robert delved into the money bag that hung at his belt. He brought out his day's takings at the pottery stall and more. "There's forty pounds here," he said. "Take this as surety. We will send the rest of the money as the king demands."

The sheriff's wife gaped openmouthed at the cheek of this man, but as she looked at the worn, ashen face of Lady Matilda, a touch of pity turned her flushed face kind. Jeweled fingers closed around the money that Robert held out.

"Go, Isabel. Take your mother home," she said quietly. "No more money will be required."

Brother James quickly carried the old woman through the noisy kitchens, Isabel at his side. Robert snatched up the plump hand of the sheriff's lady and kissed it. "This kindness shall be remembered," he whispered.

In spite of the noise and confusion that surrounded her, the sheriff's wife stared, puzzled, after the retreating backs of the potter and his lad.

They ran down the street and past the marketplace until a series of familiar whistles and the bellow of a snorting horse led them to Muchlyn, John, and the others with the potter's cart, now hidden in a blacksmith's forge close to the northern gate.

"About time!" John cried. "Can't keep this damned animal still."

Philippa ran to take Lady Matilda into her care. "Whatever have they done to you?" she cried, concerned at the old lady's frailty.

Brother James swore quietly when he saw the stamping, powerful beast that they'd taken from the castle stables. "When John steals a horse, he don't muck about," he said. "We'd best be away before this beast wakes the whole of Nottingham."

"But if we go now, we'll meet the wolf pack on the road!" cried Magda. "Isn't that right? They're heading north?"

"Yes," said Robert, with a sharp crack of laughter. "But at least they're one horse short! That'll slow them up a bit. John, you must go at once with Brother James and Philippa. Take the ladies in the cart, and make a dash for Sherwood. Hide in Bestwood Dell till they've passed. We'll catch you up."

"Aye," said John, helping to lift Matilda into the wagon. "Come, ladies. We've cloaks and straw. I hope the journey won't be too rough."

"Never mind comfort," Isabel told him, leaping up after her mother. "Just get us out of here!"

"Magda?" said John. "She should come too!"

"Nay," Robert replied, "you've got a wagonful. She'll be just as safe following with me and Tom. She can ride the potter's old nag."

John looked as though he wanted to argue, but Isabel was clearly desperate to be out of Nottingham Town.

"You take good care of my lass," said John as he snatched the reins of the wolf pack's steed and steered the wagon toward the northern gate.

8

A BUNDLE OF RAGS

ROBERT AND MAGDA emerged from the narrow close near the forge. Tom followed them, leading the potter's worn old horse, but the sound of shouting in the distance and the faint clatter of hooves made them shrink back into the darkest shadows.

Robert's arm pressed Magda against the lumpy stone walls of the blacksmith's home as the pounding of hooves and snorting of powerful horses came close. Suddenly the wolf pack was upon them . . . and passing. The streets were filled with the sound of angry voices swearing and the clink and scrape of weaponry. The wolf pack headed out of the city gate and into the night, the clamor fading until only the grumbling of the gatemen was left.

Robert relaxed. "Our turn," he said. "Get up and ride!"

"Who's this?" the guard called.

"Potter o' Mansfield and his 'prentices," Robert told him, leading the bony gray mare with Magda astride.

"Where's your wagon, then?"

"Stolen! Some great oaf! Giant of a fellow!"

The man grinned and scratched his head. "It's a bad night, right enough. Half o' Nottingham's setting out for Sherwood. I saw a wagon go tearing past awhile back, pulled

❖ 41

by some devil horse. I thought to myself, That's no potter's nag! But then the king's wolfhounds followed fast. You want no trouble with them!" The man hurriedly crossed himself.

"I'll get the thieving swine," Robert spat.

"Mind the Hooded One!" the man called out, laughing. "Watch out, or he'll be getting you."

By the time they reached the first sheltering trees, Magda was bitterly cold and weary of the jolting. The old mare stumbled through thick darkness.

"Why could I not go ahead in the wagon?" she moaned.

Robert ignored her bleating, walking in silence ahead.

Tom, who led the horse, turned to her patiently. "He has his reasons for not sending you ahead. Good reasons, I believe."

"My father wanted me to go in the wagon." Magda could hear the whine in her voice and hated it, but she was too cold and tired to stop it.

"Shall I tell her?" Tom called out to Robert.

"If you wish." Robert's uninterested voice floated back to them from the darkness ahead.

"Tell me what?" demanded Magda, suddenly warmed a little, curiosity arousing her.

"Well," said Tom. "We had to get John out of Nottingham fast, before he saw the wolf pack's leader."

"That FitzRanulf man? The one who hit me? Why should my father not see him?"

Tom went on in silence for a moment, and Robert spoke again. "She'll find out soon, anyway . . . best tell her."

With a nasty lurch of her stomach, Magda knew that she would not like what she was about to hear. "Tell me," she hissed, the jolting of the horse forgotten.

"That man, Hugh FitzRanulf," said Tom plainly. "It was

he who killed your mother. We could not let John know he was there."

The shock of hearing it numbed her; she rode on in silence, suddenly shivering, though the night was not cold.

"Magda?" Tom was anxious. "Are you all right? Did you hear me?"

"Aye." She spoke with quiet certainty. "I heard, and you were right. My father would have gone for him with his bare hands. He'd have killed him."

"Yes," Tom agreed. "Then his wolfhounds would have killed John. And if we had made a move, we'd all have been taken."

Again Robert's voice came back to them out of the darkness, oddly gentle this time. "Do you remember what I promised you, little one? There in the hall?"

"Yes," she whispered between gritted teeth. "You said that death should not be good enough for FitzRanulf."

They traveled on through the darkness, for Robert insisted that they were not safe on the outskirts of the forest.

Magda rode in thoughtful silence for a while, but weariness caught up with her. "We're miles from Nottingham now," she complained. "How does Robert know where we're safe and where we are not?"

"He knows," said Tom. "Eyes like a fox he has, and ears too."

At last Robert turned about. "This'll do. Sleep now," he said. "We'll wake at dawn and go to find John."

"Can we make a fire?" Magda asked.

"No," Robert told her. "We're not far enough from town for that."

"But I'm cold," she whispered.

"Here's a fine patch of dry, springy moss," said Robert,

kicking around in the undergrowth. "Come wrap that cloak around and snuggle down between the two of us. Not every little lass has two fine fellows like us to keep her warm! Eh, Tom?"

"Aye." She could hear the answering laughter in Tom's voice.

"I'm not a little lass," she said, wishing Robert would go away and leave her there beside Tom. But she did as she was told, making sure that she settled down on Robert's left side.

"There. Warm and safe?" Robert asked.

"Yes," she answered, grudgingly comforted by the warmth of two strong male bodies and the familiar woodland sounds.

It was not the morning light that wakened them but the faint creak and rumble of a cart. Robert and Tom were at once alert and ready to jump. A low bellow in the distance was answered by a whicker from the potter's horse, then came a small thud.

"What is it?" Magda whispered.

"Hush!" Robert hissed. "Be still. An ox and cart, I think . . . but it's moving away."

They crouched in silence, peering through dim light that showed them the muzzy shapes of trees, but nothing moved.

"You sleep again," Robert told them. "I'll watch."

"I can't," said Magda. "I'm wide awake now."

"They dropped something," Tom insisted. "I want to know what."

Magda watched him tread soundlessly through the grass and then crouch to peer closely at a bush. Suddenly sharp clattering arose, sending rooks screeching from the trees.

Tom leapt backward. Robert and Magda were both ready to run, but Tom quickly recovered and called to them.

"Nowt to fear. Come here!"

Magda went cautiously toward him, but all she could see through the gloom was a bundle of rags dumped beneath the bush. As she stepped closer, the bundle moved, and a thin white hand wagged a noisy wooden clapper in the air, making her cry out in alarm.

Robert grabbed Magda by the arm and pulled her back.

"Tom!" he cried. "Keep away! A leper!"

Magda's heart thudded with fear at his words. Was that the meaning of the harsh clapper? She'd never come across the disease, not in all her years with the Forestwife, though she'd heard enough about it to dread it.

"Get back, Tom!" she yelled.

But Tom did not retreat again. He bent down toward the bundled rags. " 'Tis but a child," he murmured.

"Do not touch! Do not touch!" Magda screamed it frantically at him. She went slowly to see for herself, then caught her breath. She looked down through the faint dawning light on the pinched face of the Nottingham potter's boy, a dark bruise showing on his chin where she had hit him.

❧9❧

BESTWOOD DELL

MAGDA REMEMBERED the strange red patch on the boy's throat and his frantic search for herbs.

"Look!" she told Robert. "See who it is! He was with the potter in the next stall."

Robert scratched his head. "The lad you sent flying? Aye, so it is. What are you doing here, boy?" he asked.

The boy sat mute and still as a statue, staring blankly; he would not look at them. When Tom held out his hand, he quickly snatched up the clapper and set it snapping its harsh rhythm through the quiet trees.

"Stop it!" Magda cried, covering her ears with her hands. "I hate it."

There was silence again until Tom spoke. "But you are no leper," he said. "Surely?"

Then in a small, shaky whisper, the boy answered. "Father says I am."

"Why?" Magda cried. "Why should he think it so?"

"My mother was stricken soon after my birth," the boy whispered.

Magda shivered.

"Where is your mother? Does she live?" Tom asked.

"Stoned." The lad spoke without emotion. "The villagers

stoned her. Father says it is best that I go, seek out my own kind. Better than suffer my mother's fate."

"Your father!" Robert almost spat it out. "Was that he?" he asked, pointing after the cart.

The boy nodded.

"I cannot believe it," Tom cried. "You are no leper! Magda, tell him so!"

But Magda could not forget the sight of the patchy red skin. She shook her head. "I don't know," she said. "His skin is marked."

Tom stood up. "We must give him food and let him have the horse," he said.

"That was for me." Magda heard her own voice sounding pettish.

Robert shook his head, uncertain for once. "Give him the horse, but he'd best keep his distance from us. I'm sorry for the lad, but we've troubles enough of our own. We must eat and find ourselves water and be on our way." Suddenly his expression was lighter. With a flourish he brought out a loaf of fine white bread from his potter's sack. "A gift from our sheriff's lady."

"It cheers you to think you've cheated anyone," Magda declared.

"Only rich fools," Robert laughed.

They divided up the loaf, and Tom carried a good hunk over to the potter's boy. His hands closed about the soft white bread that was such a treat, but he seemed unable to eat. Tom crouched down, full of comforting words, but Magda was quickly on her feet and shouting furiously again. "Do not touch him!"

When at last they were ready to go, Tom held the bridle and soothed the horse while the lad obediently struggled to mount. He accepted the reins without thanks. Tom slapped the bony flank, and the horse set off north toward Barnsdale, the boy sitting stiffly astride like a straw-stuffed doll.

Tom watched him go, a troubled expression on his face.

"There's nowt we can do," Robert told him, shaking his head.

"He says his name is Alan—same as my grandfather," Tom said.

When at last the potter's son was out of sight, Robert made them walk northwest, along one of his secret paths, heading for Bestwood Dell. There was no sign of the wagon at the dell, just Brother James settled on a rock and John striding back and forth, crushing a pathway of thick green bracken beneath his feet, his face like thunder.

As soon as the big man heard their approach, he leapt across the small clearing, whipping his meat knife from his belt. "You crafty whippet, you lying hound," he growled, grabbing a fistful of jerkin and thrusting the knife at Robert's throat. Brother James hurriedly got up from his rock.

For a moment Magda was frightened, but Robert's silence was reassuring. He stood there white-faced, blinking up at his friend, but he would not give ground.

"You kept the bastard from me," John spat at him. "You took my daughter in there! You sat my child down before her mother's murderer!"

Magda kept still and quiet, but remembered with resentment. Aye, and he let him hit me about the head, she thought.

Even though John prodded at his neck with the sharp point of his knife till a trickle of blood ran, Robert did not speak. "I could have killed the man!" John roared. "I could have torn him apart!"

Still Robert said nothing, but Tom went slowly to stand

at his side and face John. "We don't doubt that you would have killed him," he said. "But then what? I think Robert did right to keep you in ignorance."

Magda lurched toward her father, but she dared not grab his arm. Though she knew he loved her dearly, he was still a huge and very angry man. "Robert has promised—" she said, swallowing hard to stop her voice shaking. "Robert has promised me this FitzRanulf shall be punished. Look at me, Father! Did you want to lose me too?"

John turned to her, and his face crumpled. He swung around and threw down the knife with so much force that it buried itself up to the hilt in the grassy earth. He crouched down amid the bracken, covering his face with his hands. Magda went to him and wrapped her arms about his shoulders.

The others watched solemnly.

"Leave them," said Brother James. "Let them grieve. Old wounds bleed afresh. Come here! I've something to show you." Brother James waved Robert and Tom over to the rock that he'd been sitting on.

"Where's the wagon?" Robert asked. "And Lady Matilda?"

"Philippa insisted on taking Isabel and Matilda straight home," Brother James told him. "Muchlyn and Stoutley went with them. Matilda looks poorly. A frail old woman should not be dragged away from her hearthside like that. Our king would steal the gold from a dying man if he thought he could get but a pennyworth. The thought of Isabel wed to that wolfhound of his makes me shiver."

"Yes," said Robert thoughtfully. "We've bought the girl a bit of time, but we shall have to think long and hard about it. Even if we can manage to raise the money he demands, the man never keeps to his word. Once King John has dealt

with the lady de Braose, he'll remember this other Matilda—
and he's in such a rage, God knows what he'll do."

The fat face of Brother James lit up with excitement.
"Matilda . . . de . . . Braose." He said the words slowly and
with pleasure. "I have a wild idea that might teach the king
what true rage is!"

⟨10⟩

THE BRAVEST
WOMAN IN THE LAND

ROBERT WAS INSTANTLY excited and smiled hugely. "Why, damn it, Brother James!" he cried. "Is this one of your crazy plans? I need something mad and risky to cheer me."

"What's this?" Tom frowned down at a muddle of scratched lines and marks upon the rock.

"It's a map," Brother James told them. "Though only clever learned folk like me can read it."

Robert threw a mock punch at his face. "All right, all right! Explain it to us poor fools."

Brother James pointed with a dirty finger. "Now see this line here, the Great North Road, and this patch here, Barnsdale Waste, and here that dip in the land where the River Went runs."

"Our favorite spot for bishop baiting," remarked Tom.

John and Magda came slowly to join them, calmed a little and intrigued by Brother James's excitement.

"What's this you're plotting now?" John asked.

"A rescue." Brother James spoke so fast that tiny beads of spit flew from his lips. "A rescue that will stagger the king."

"Steady on," said Tom, wiping his eye. "You'll have drowned us all before we're done."

Brother James ignored him, waving his hands wildly. "Don't you see? We have a bit of time to make a plan, for it will take those foul wolfhounds a sennight to reach the Scottish borders and then start back again."

"What?" Robert asked. "You'd have us set upon the wolf pack?"

"Wherever they are taking the lady de Braose, they will have to travel the Great North Road and pass through Barnsdale." Brother James wagged a finger in Robert's face. "That is where they are weak and we are strong."

"I'm for it!" said John at once. "It'll give me a chance to get my hands on FitzRanulf."

"It's the woman I'm after," said Brother James.

"What do you want with her?" Robert asked, amazed. "When have we bothered with mighty lords and their wives?"

Brother James's face was red with concern. "She's the bravest woman in the land."

It was dusk when they began crossing the wilder scrubland at the edge of Barnsdale Waste, and Magda was exhausted. Robert and Brother James marched steadily ahead of them, discussing their plans with wild enthusiasm. The truth was that Magda longed for the comfort of her sweet-smelling straw pallet and Marian's glowing fire. A faint *clop, clop* of horse hooves made Tom whistle a quick warning, and without further fuss they all melted into a ditch.

John gently pushed Magda's head down beneath the cover of a holly bush, but then she felt her father relax. "Just one horse," he whispered, "and nowt but a stringy bairn."

Magda got up with John and recognized the pathetic rider at once. "Oh no," she sighed, somehow irritated. "Not him again. We gave him the horse! Isn't that enough?"

Robert, Tom, and Brother James climbed out of the ditch

and joined them. Tom went forward to meet the boy, but though he stood there staring up into Alan's face, the lad made no attempt to halt. Tom dived to the side to avoid the horse's trampling hooves, then quickly recovered and ran after it, snatching at its bridle. "Whoa!" he shouted.

The old nag stopped willingly enough when bidden, but Magda warned the others off. "Leper!" she cried. "Beware!"

Quietly they gathered about the rider, keeping a good arm's distance away. The boy's face was white and blank, his eyes focused far beyond them on the road ahead.

"Alan." Tom spoke gently. "Where have you been? You set off far ahead of us."

No answer came. No response of any kind.

"He set off north," Tom told them. "How has he taken so long? What is wrong?"

They all looked up again at the small figure. Magda thought him as lifeless as a statue she'd seen in the great hall of Nottingham Castle. If it was not that he sat so straight and still clutched the reins, he might be dead.

Brother James patted the steaming rump of the potter's mare. "I think this old lass has been in charge," he said. "I daresay she's been taking her chance to feed on marsh-watered grass, but now she wants warm stabling, so she heads for her home in Mansfield."

"Aye." Robert smiled. "The lad has sat like a moppet, and never taken charge."

Brother James shook his head sadly. "I fear that this poor lad can take charge of naught."

11

None Shall Be
Turned Away

"WE SHOULD TAKE HIM to Marian," said Tom.

"What?" Magda cried. "And risk ourselves?"

Robert and John were both silent, worried by Tom's suggestion.

Brother James shook his head. "I know naught of leprosy," he said. "But Mother Veronica does."

They all turned to stare at him, surprised. Mother Veronica and the Sisters of the Magdalen lived close to Langden, quietly caring for the sick and needy around them.

"The nuns have never had lepers in their care," said Magda.

"No, not here in the wastes." Brother James smiled with amusement. "But Veronica was not always a nun. She's traveled widely! Why, when she was just a young lass, she was maid to King John's mother. Eleanor of Aquitaine went off over sea and land to Outremer with her first husband, the young French king. Veronica went with them."

"You mean Mother Veronica went to Jerusalem? Following the crusaders?" Robert was amazed.

"You sound a touch envious!" said John.

"I thought they'd always been there in the woods," said Magda. It was very hard to see fat, bossy Mother Veronica as an adventurous young woman traveling with foreign kings and the famous Queen Eleanor.

"There's much you do not know about Mother Veronica." Brother James chuckled. "She was once betrothed to a brave knight, but she never married him. Veronica refused to follow her mistress back home to France, so they parted company. She stayed out there in those strange heathen lands for many years, helping to set up a hospital for lepers."

There was a moment of silence while they struggled to fix this new picture of the nun in their minds.

"So, what of this lad?" Tom was determined to make them think of the present. "We're not far from Langden now."

"There are leper hospitals here in England," said Brother James. "I believe there's one at York."

"He looks half dead anyway," Magda muttered.

James turned to her and spoke rather sternly. "I think it only Christian and decent that we at least take him with us to the Forestwife."

Magda frowned and felt mean. Truth was, she was desperate to get home now.

"Aye," Robert agreed. "We can all keep our distance from him. Let the poor fellow follow behind us. We'd best not call in at Langden—they've trouble enough."

"You go on ahead," Tom insisted. "I'll lead Alan's horse. I swear he knows nowt of what's going on."

They set off again as fast as they could, hoping to reach the Forestwife's clearing before the light went. As they trudged through the gloom, Madga longed to be home. Her feet were sore, but she knew that each step brought her closer to her familiar woodland. She had had enough of adventuring for the moment. Even the muddy, sappy smell comforted her.

"Not far now," her father soothed. "Shall I carry thee?"

Magda shook her head. It would be shameful to arrive back from her first outing into the world beyond Barnsdale carried—especially in front of Tom. She turned to look for him as they reached the secret maze of paths that protected the Forestwife's clearing. She stared, puzzled, though it was hard to see in the failing light. The horse plowed on with the silhouette of the lad above. Magda could see no sign of Tom.

"Tom! Where is he?" she cried.

John turned around, screwing up his eyes to see better. Then as the horse plodded toward them, they saw the dark shape of Tom riding behind the leper boy. He was supporting him, arms around the lad's waist, the reins in his hands. Magda was so shocked that she could not speak. The blood drained from her face. She and John stared, horrified.

As the horse came close, Magda could only whisper, "Why, Tom? Why? You have put us all at risk!"

"He has given up all hope," Tom told her. "I came to the Forestwife like him, my life in tatters. Though I was only a child, and it was long ago, I can't forget it!"

"Thank goodness, you're back!" Marian's voice rang out clear, and a flickering light showed through the dark trees. She strode toward them from the shadows, carrying a lantern high.

"Aye," Robert answered her. "We're all back safe, but I fear we've brought more worries with us. See what this mad fellow has done." Robert pointed to Tom.

Marian shielded her eyes to see better. "Is that Tom?"

"Aye," said Robert. "And we believe the lad to be leprous."

"He's gone mad," cried Magda. "It's bad enough that Tom insists we bring the boy here, but then he goes and climbs up on the horse with him. He'll make lepers of us all!"

Marian frowned and moved closer as the horse nickered, and stopped. "I know Tom," she said. "He does naught without good reason."

Tom's face was pale in the lantern's light. He shrugged his shoulders.

Brother James went to put his arm around Marian. "Mother Veronica knows much of the disease," he said. "I thought perhaps she could help."

"It seemed hard to leave the lad," John agreed. "He's nowt but a bairn. It seems his father carried him out to the woods and left him outcast. I know the man's right by law, but it's a bitter decree that makes a father throw out his child."

Marian lifted the lantern until it lit Alan's blank, still face. "What is your name?" she asked.

There was no reply.

"He is called Alan," said Tom. "He's too fearful even to speak."

Marian gave a great sigh, but then she spoke solemnly. "Of those who seek the Forestwife, none shall be turned away."

"I hope you know what you do," said Robert thoughtfully. "Does not the law say lepers must be cast out?"

"And does that trouble you?" Marian feigned astonishment.

Robert suddenly laughed and kissed her. "You are right, sweetheart. He's one of us! We might as well add another small crime to our great list!"

"Aye." Marian sighed. "Tom, will you take Alan and the

horse round to the shelter at the back. There's straw to make a bed, and I shall bring rugs and food. And Tom, I fear . . ."

"Aye," said Tom. "I know. I'll stay there with him."

Marian nodded. "We'll send for Mother Veronica at dawn."

There was a great to-do getting everyone fed and warm inside the small hut, but the old one had the fire built up and a great pot of mutton stew bubbling above it. It was only when they had eaten their fill and wiped their bowls with fresh-baked bread that they began to tell what had happened in Nottingham.

"So, do you think Matilda and Isabel are safe?" Marian asked.

"Safe for a time," Robert told her. "The king has a greater Matilda to worry about now, and Brother James has a wild idea of rescue in his head. So crazy a plan that I warm to the thought of it."

Marian smiled. "I thought I knew that gleam in your eye."

"If we could succeed, it would delight all of England," said Brother James. "It would make the king a laughing-stock."

Marian listened well as they told her how the king had sent the wolf pack off to the Scottish borders to take captive the lady de Braose.

"Aye," Marian agreed. "Though she was once rich and powerful, I do honor her actions. She's lost all she had by defying the king, and she's done it in defense of her children. She is a good mother—I'll give her that."

Magda went to her straw pallet and snuggled beneath her goatskin rug. Even Marian seemed keen for this new scheme of theirs. Magda could not share their interest; she was still angry with Tom, though she could not quite work out why.

As the fire died down, one by one the company fell asleep until, besides Magda, only Robert and Marian remained awake. At last they went to Marian's pallet and settled down together for the night. Magda could hear Marian laughing softly. She turned over so that she could not see them anymore. Marian had not laughed like that for a long time. I suppose she'll be singing in the morning, Magda thought.

12

AN AWKWARD MAN

MAGDA DID NOT SLEEP well and crept outside at the first touch of dawn. She stumbled around to the spring behind the cottage as darkness slowly lifted from the sheltering yew trees, but someone was there at the spring before her.

"Tom?" she called.

"Aye." He dipped a wooden bowl into the the clean, warm springwater that bubbled up from the rocks at the heart of the Forestwife's clearing.

Magda crouched beside him and splashed water onto her face, then as Tom stepped back toward the shelter with a full bowl, she remembered Alan. Her stomach tightened with fear. "Don't you let him touch this water!" she cried. "He might foul it all up with his disease."

Tom nodded. "That's why I take water to him."

Magda watched as he carefully carried water into the lean-to and listened as he woke the boy, speaking gently to him. Then she heard a faint and husky reply.

Magda sighed and returned to the cottage. Marian was awake and looking for her.

"Will you run to Mother Veronica and fetch her to look at that poor lad?"

Magda made a face. "Can't Tom go?"

"I think it best Tom stay by Alan's side until we hear what Mother Veronica has to say. Besides," said Marian, touching Magda's cheek, "there's none that can run as fast through the secret tracks as you, and the sooner we know how to care for the boy the better, don't you think?"

Magda had to agree. The sooner they were rid of him, the happier she would be, so she pulled on Tom's breeches again and laced on her strong leather boots. "I think I like men's clothes," she said more cheerfully. "Better for running in."

The sun gave sharp light and good warmth as Magda went through the woods. Her spirits soared as she ran like a hare through dew-laden grass, past branches of trembling hazel catkins. As she neared the forest convent of the Magdalen, she found that a fine carpet of bluebells covered the ground. She drew in deep lungfuls of scented air. The rich sights and smells of Nottingham Town had nothing to equal this.

Magda arrived at the convent breathless and hungry. Sister Rosamund took one look at her and quickly served up warm fresh bread and goat cheese with a mug of the nuns' thin ale. Mother Veronica sat at the table and listened as Magda gasped out the story of Alan.

The old nun shook her head. "Poor boy, poor boy!" she said.

"But he'll make us all sick like him!" Magda cried. "Even the law says it . . . lepers must live apart from healthy folk."

Mother Veronica shook her head. "Aye, but there's much within the law that is unjust. Believe me, child," she said, taking Magda's hand, "there is no need for all this fear. I spent seven years living with lepers and caring for them. I did not catch the disease, nor did any who worked alongside of me. We must be careful not to touch leprous sores or share food or eat from their bowls, but that is all."

"I hit him with my fist," Magda cried, clenching her fist again.

"Poor boy," repeated Mother Veronica.

"But will I get leprosy?"

The nun smiled and shook her head.

Magda had a sudden picture of Tom carrying the bowl of water to Alan. "Eat from their bowls? Drink from their bowls? But what if Tom—?"

"Stop it," said Mother Veronica firmly. "We will go straight to see this fellow, then I can tell you more."

ALAN MEEKLY allowed Mother Veronica to examine his face and limbs. All the company waited anxiously outside the lean-to shelter.

"Fetch me a needle!" Mother Veronica demanded.

Marian brought a rusty iron needle from the hut. Mother Veronica cleaned the point and lightly pricked the red patches of skin. The boy did not flinch.

"Ah," said Mother Veronica. "Yes. I fear it is leprosy, but the disease is young. There is no contagion as yet from these patches of skin. Tom, you are quite safe."

"Thank goodness," said Marian.

But Magda was not so easily satisfied. "Did you eat or drink from his bowl?" she demanded.

Tom shook his head.

Magda's eyes suddenly filled with tears of relief; she dashed them hurriedly away.

Mother Veronica took off her cloak and wrapped it around Alan's shoulders. "With good feeding and care we may hold the sickness back and keep him strong. There is an oil—a precious oil that we used in the lands of Outremer. It came from far away to the east, beyond Jerusalem, but we cannot get it here."

"Does it cure?" asked Marian, interested as ever in healing skills.

Mother Veronica shook her head. "No, but it seemed to help. If he'll come, I shall take the child back with me to the sisters. We will do all we can for him."

Alan looked worried. "Will you come too?" he begged Tom.

"Of course." Tom nodded.

Magda was relieved, though she wished Tom didn't have to go off with them. Alan seemed to watch him like a faithful puppy dog. Marian agreed to the arrangement, for the Forestwife had misery and sickness enough to deal with in the secret clearing in Barnsdale Forest.

Magda stood with Marian by the turning stone, waving them off. "I hope Mother Veronica is right," she said. "I hope we are all safe from contagion!"

"Mother Veronica is always right," Marian told her sharply.

Magda looked surprised at such sharpness. "What are you angry about?" she asked. "We are saved from leprosy, and I thought you'd be happy, now that he's back." She nodded toward the cottage, where she supposed Robert still slept.

"He?" Marian said. "Have you not noticed? He's taken that horse and gone."

"So soon? Where?"

Marian shrugged her shoulders. "Who knows? I have no time to worry over him. There's herbs to brew for a woman with dropsy, and a lad with a poisoned wound to clean.

You should do your shooting practice. Who knows what may come next! Don't let your visit to Nottingham make you grow slack!"

"Is my father . . . ?"

"Aye, don't fret. Your father cuts yew staves round by the shelter."

Magda went gladly to help John with the task he'd set for himself.

"Just what I need," said John. "A fine strapping lad to help me!"

She smiled at his teasing for, beneath his jokes, she knew that he was proud of her strength and skill with a knife.

"Marian insists on shooting practice," Magda complained.

"She's right," John told her. "Shooting practice could save your life, honey. Come help me with these staves, then I'll fetch my own bow and go along with you."

"Why does Robert make Marian so miserable?" Magda asked. "I swear I would not take up with a man like him. He blows hot and cold all the time."

John put his arm around his daughter's shoulders and sighed. "It is not just Marian on whom he blows hot and cold. The man is that way and he cannot change himself. I think the bitterness of this world hangs very heavy on him. When we are out in the woods and wastes, he will often slip into a foul mood and never speak to us for days. Then he'll go off alone, and believe me, we are glad to see the back of him."

"Where does he go?"

John shook his head. "Derbyshire, Loxley, Sheaf Valley . . . who knows? Sometimes he comes back smelling of salt, with a sack full of seaweed for Marian."

"I wondered how she kept her supplies so well stocked. But how does he find you again?"

John laughed. "We leave our secret signs: knots in branches, pebbles on the ground. He tracks us through the woods and catches up with us when it suits him. He'll suddenly turn up, wild with plans for some reckless scheme and full of love for us."

"He's such an awkward man!" said Magda. "How can you be his friend?"

"When he is happy, he is the best fellow in the world," said John. "There is nothing he will not attempt, nothing he will not dare. I love him like a brother."

Magda sighed, for she could not understand, but she worked on with her father until the sun was high in the sky. After they'd eaten, they took their bows and enjoyed a shooting match that Magda won, though she suspected that John let her.

When they wandered back to the hut, they found Marian scraping fresh-cut herbs from a wooden bowl onto the hearthstone to dry, her knife rattling fast and angry.

"No sign of him, I suppose?"

John touched her shoulder. "You chose the wrong man if you wanted a tame house cat."

"Aye," said Marian, wiping her hands and her knife. "I chose the wrong man! I chose the wrong place! I chose the wrong life!"

The old one came into the hut, her arms full of elder flowers. She gasped as she heard her daughter's words.

Marian dropped her knife and ran to hug her, crushing the flowers. "No, Mother! I am sorry. It is just that man! I would not change you for the world."

"Good to see someone pleased with life!" said Robert,

ducking his head and stepping across the threshold. He was rid of the clay-spattered clothes and wore his own faded cloak and close-fitting hood.

"Where have you been?" Marian demanded.

"To Langden, of course. I thought the potter deserved to get his horse back, and I wanted to speak to Philippa's husband. We shall need a good blacksmith if we are to rescue this poor Lady de Braose. We shall need swords, knives, arrowheads. And Philippa's man's the best I know!" He grabbed Marian around the waist and kissed her cheek. "What do you think, sweetheart?"

"I wish you would tell me where you go," she said.

◄§13§►

A DEFIANT
COMPANY

OVER THE NEXT few days the clearing was filled with
activity. Much, Brother James, and Will Stoutley went off
with messages to hamlets and villages where they knew
they had friends. Robert and John marched back and forth
between the woods and Langden, carrying weapons and
new-made arrow tips from Philippa's blacksmith husband.

"There will be many to feed," the old one said, and she
worked hard producing oatcakes and stews of peas and
beans, flavored with garlic and a little venison.

Slowly a great company gathered. Dusty-skinned coal
diggers left their shallow bell pits, and soot-blackened
charcoal burners set their stacks aside. Shepherds and swine-
herds left their flocks with their children, and strong-built
woodlanders left their coppicing, for they'd many grievances
against the king, and the defiance of the de Braose family
was admired.

"What is it that this woman has done?" Magda asked as
she pounded grain with Marian and Eleanor.

"William de Braose was the king's friend," Eleanor told
her. "So close a friend, it seems he knows too much. He
owed the king money, so, as usual, King John demanded

the family send their son to him as hostage. Well, Matilda de Braose refused."

"She did more than that," said Marian. "She declared to all who'd listen that she'd not let her son suffer the same fate as Arthur of Brittany!"

"Arthur?" said Magda. "Do you mean King John's nephew?"

"That's the one," Marian agreed. "You know what happened to him?"

Magda was puzzled. "Did he die?"

Marian shook her head sadly. "Rumor has it that the king strangled the boy with his own hands."

Magda stopped her pounding. "Do you think that true?"

"If anyone knows the truth, it is Matilda de Braose. Her husband was there in the castle in France when Arthur disappeared."

"But isn't William de Braose a powerful lord?"

"He was," said Eleanor. "He's a fugitive now—as much as any of these lads here in the wastes."

"Do you think they can rescue the lady? Can you see what will be, old one?"

Eleanor shook her head and smiled. "I can't see that, dear heart. But whether they succeed or not, at least they are strong and defiant while they try."

Magda begged her father to take her with them, but John would not hear of it. "This is the most dangerous task we've taken upon ourselves," he said. "And I am going to get FitzRanulf! I cannot be worrying about my child."

"But Philippa and Mother Veronica go with you!"

"Aye, for we must have someone the lady will trust."

The afternoon that Robert, John, and Tom went, they packed up bundles of smoked venison and dried oatcakes, for they'd need their strength. The company would leave at dusk so that they could move through the woodlands under the protection of darkness. Then they'd set up camp within view of the Great North Road.

Tom, back from the convent, packed his food, then told Robert that he would not be going with them.

Robert looked surprised but listened carefully to what Tom had to say.

"Mother Veronica believes there may be a source of that rare oil Alan needs."

"Where?" Magda asked.

"Up beyond Doncaster, not far from Wakefield, there is a place called Temple Newhouse."

"Do you mean the preceptory?"

Tom nodded. "That's the place."

"The Templar knights? You'd go calling on them?"

Marian frowned. "I begin to see," she said. "If anyone has brought back medicines from those distant lands, it would be the strange fighting monks."

Robert drew in his breath sharply. "Be careful, Tom. Those men are fierce fighters and a law unto themselves; even the king cannot control them."

"Sounds just like us," said John.

"Don't go," cried Magda. "Why risk yourself?"

"Everything we do is a risk." Tom shrugged his shoulders. "Robert goes chasing off to risk himself for a brave lady. I go for Alan. Besides"—he smiled—"Mother Veronica has given me a letter that she swears will keep me safe. Walter of Stainthorpe is a powerful Templar knight, and he is the man she was once to marry."

"Ah!" Marian understood.

"They may not have the oil, but I must try," Tom insisted.

"Fair enough," said Robert. "I wish you well."

When they had gone, the clearing seemed quiet and dreary. Though the usual procession of sick people and animals came and went, Magda was restless and dull. She went about her chores, fetching wood, picking berries and herbs, cutting rushes, and digging latrines.

One afternoon, as she set out laden with baskets and sacks, she caught a glimpse of a small figure dashing behind a tree. Magda dropped her bags and ran lightly toward the place. Behind a thick elder bush she found a young girl with mud-smudged cheeks and a bloodstained skirt. She clutched a dead-looking gray dog in her arms.

Magda sighed. This was a common sight in the clearing. She bent down and lightly touched the dog's dangling right paw, which was wrapped in a dirty rag.

"Regarders caught our Fetcher . . . chasing deer," the girl whispered. "They came and lamed him." She shook so much that she could hardly be heard.

"What?" said Magda. "Speak up!"

"The Forestwife. I seek the wise woman's help."

"Too late." Magda spoke sadly. "I think your Fetcher's dead." She pushed her fingers into the rough fur of the dog's neck and felt a faint pulse beat. "Oh well," she said. "You'd best follow me. Where have you come from?"

"Clipstone, within the bounds of Sherwood." The girl struggled to her feet, and Magda took the dog from her.

"He's a weight, all right," she said kindly. "How have you managed him? How old are you?"

"Twelve last birthday."

"You've come a long way, and he's lost a lot of blood. I don't know that we can save him. What's your name?"

"Joanna."

"Are you hungry?"

The girl nodded, but suddenly stopped.

"What's wrong?"

"I'm feared. Feared of the Forestwife and the man, the Hooded One."

Magda could not help but smile, remembering what she'd heard in Nottingham of the fearful Witch of Barnsdale.

"Come with me and don't be feared. The Forestwife is my mother . . . well, she's all the mother I've got. She lives here with Eleanor, the old one. And as for the Hooded One, he's away from here just now."

A touch of curiosity showed on Joanna's face, and she allowed herself to be led into the clearing to Marian. While Magda told Joanna's story, the girl stared quietly up at the tall woman in the worn homespun gown with the beautiful woven girdle.

Marian made them put Fetcher by the hearthstone and sent them to bring water from the spring to wash his wound. "He's very weak," she said, "but a few scraps of meat and our good springwater can sometimes work wonders."

·≪14≫·

THE RETURN

JOANNA WOULD NOT leave Fetcher's side; she brought him water and fed him scraps of meat by hand. It was slow work, but the big, rough dog did not die in the night as they'd feared. On the third day he looked much better, and though he still could not get to his feet, he whimpered and licked Joanna's hand.

"Take the lass out for a walk," Eleanor told Magda. "She's sat by that beast too long."

"Yes," said Marian. "Take her and go to visit the sisters. Ask if they've heard aught of Robert's gang."

It took a bit of persuading, but once the two girls were out in the sunshine, striding through the bluebells, Joanna began to look happier.

"Won't be long now," said Magda. "Then you can take him home."

"I'm not sure I can find the way again," Joanna said. "Maybe I can stay here with you?"

"But what of your parents?" asked Magda. "Are they kind to you?"

"Mother shouts and Father sends me out in the cold for firewood," said Joanna.

"Huh!" muttered Magda. "That's what Marian does to me! Will they be worried?"

The girl looked thoughtful. "Aye, they will. Mother will cry and Father will be looking and looking for me."

"Then I think you should go back," said Magda. "My father will take you. He'll take you as soon as he returns."

Sister Rosamund welcomed them to the convent kitchen and brought them bread and small ale. She shook her head and looked worried when they asked for news of Robert. "Mother Veronica should never have gone," she said. "She's getting too old to go rushing around the countryside with a great gang of outcast fellows."

"I suppose you think you should have gone instead," said Magda cheekily.

Sister Rosamund laughed and nodded her head

As they left, Magda noticed a small hut set a little apart from the main convent building, newly thatched and paneled, surrounded by bluebells.

"What have you made there?" Magda asked.

Sister Rosamund sighed. "Alan," she said. "The poor leper lad. We've set him up there among the bluebells to cheer him, but he waits like a little lost dog for Tom's return."

Joanna shuddered at the mention of the disease.

Magda sighed. "Come on," she said. "I suppose we'd better go and see him." She grabbed Joanna's arm and walked over to the hut.

Alan was staring into the distance, his thin arms folded still and statuelike in his lap. At last he looked up at his visitors, and suddenly recognition showed in his face. "I thought you were a lad," he said to Magda.

"Aye," said Magda. "I can fight you!"

Alan rubbed his chin. All bruising had gone. "Yes, you

can," he agreed. "I knew I could never really be a squire."

"No," said Magda. "But if it's possible to get this special oil, Tom will find it for you."

The two girls walked back through the woods, both quiet and deep in thought, but as they neared the Forestwife's clearing, something made Magda uneasy. She stopped and grabbed Joanna's hand.

"What is it?" Joanna whispered.

Magda shook her head. "Too still, too quiet," she said. "No birds, no squirrels—and look at the path."

Though the earth was dry, there were footprints and scuff marks on it as though an army had passed that way.

Joanna picked up a piece of brown, blood-soaked rag.

"Was that from your Fetcher?" Magda asked.

Joanna shook her head, then they heard the sound of men's voices and the clink of weapons.

"Careful," Magda warned. "Get off the path!"

The two girls crept away from the open space and hid for a moment in the undergrowth. Nobody came, but they could hear the sound of voices.

"They're in the clearing," said Magda. She put her finger to her lips.

Joanna followed her along a deep and secret way that brought them up beside the sweeping branches of the great yews. It was men's voices that they'd heard, but pitifully groaning and whimpering. Magda heard Marian calling for food and water. They pushed the branches aside and saw the most dreadful sight. The soft green turf was littered with wounded men. Marian and Eleanor strode back and forth among them with water, clean rags, and ointments. Mother Veronica was there, her habit dirty and torn. She saw the two girls and beckoned them through.

"What is it?" Magda asked, her voice shaking with fear. "Is my father . . . ?"

"He's got a clout and a wounded leg," Mother Veronica told her quickly. "But he'll be fine. Now come, we need your help! They've struggled back without food or water. Can you run to the convent and get the sisters to come? Ask Sister Rosamund to bring her bundles and potions. We need food and ale and clean rags!"

Magda sighed at the thought of the journey she'd just made, but she nodded. "Is the lady saved?" she asked.

Robert's bitter voice answered her. "She is not!"

Magda ran back faster than ever and brought the nuns and their supplies. Isabel had been visiting Sister Rosamund and insisted that she come along with the nuns to help. They worked hard through the rest of the day, and by nightfall the men were all fed and made as comfortable as possible, their wounds cleaned and bandaged and wrapped in warm rags. Philippa sat under the trysting tree, her face as pale as water, Much's head in her lap.

"It's a good thing we're not caught like this in freezing winter weather," Eleanor said, building up the fire.

Robert sat hunched and gloomy by the hearthside, refusing to lie down and rest though he'd a long sword cut on his good cheek and painful smashed ribs. "What's this mutt?" he asked, pointing at Fetcher, who'd crept quietly into the shadows and was watching the activity with new fear.

Brother James turned to look into the darkness at the edges of the cottage.

"That's my dog, Fetcher." Joanna spoke out fearlessly. "Who are you?"

Robert answered through gritted teeth. "I am . . . I was . . . the Hooded One."

⤜15⤏

THE KNIGHTS OF SAINT LAZARUS

SLOWLY, BIT BY BIT, the story was told. The men had made camp at Wentbridge by the Great North Road and set a lookout for the closed wagon that would carry Matilda de Braose and her son. They'd just begun to run out of food when three closed wagons, escorted by the wolf pack, were spied. The band of outlaws had hesitated, but only for a moment. Though the king's mercenaries were heavily armed, Robert's lads were fired up and guessed they outnumbered them.

Robert led a fierce attack, but while the first wagon was hurried on, the second two proved to be packed with armed foot soldiers, who leapt out onto the outlaws. The rebels had made a bitter fight of it, but they had not had a chance against so many. FitzRanulf had ridden away fast with the leading wagon. John had found himself in the middle of thick fighting, unable to leave his friends to pursue his own quarrel.

Fifteen lads had been killed outright, and every one of the others carried some hurt. Though the women worked hard to save them, five more died in the night. One of them was Muchlyn.

John sat by the fire with Robert, growling out his anger.

"The blasted coward! Could not stay and fight but runs off, leaving his men to do his dirty work."

Robert's face was gray, his scar standing out livid, and streaked with fresh cuts.

Somehow John knew that his friend needed comfort more than he. "We made ourselves felt!" he said. "Much would be proud to go in such a fight. We cut that gang of mercenaries down to half!"

Robert would not answer or allow himself to be tended.

Marian walked back and forth with a face like stone. She worked all day and most of the night, feeding, cleaning, making up simples and poultices. Magda and Joanna did all they could to help; the miserable plight of the men gave them the energy to carry on with little food or sleep. Magda did not even complain at the hated job of digging latrines— it was better than digging graves!

Three more died, though at least their pain was soothed by Marian's sleeping drafts. At last, when six days had passed, those who could walk began to leave the clearing, and Eleanor insisted that Marian sleep. When she woke, Robert was gone, his place by the hearth taken by Fetcher. Magda and Joanna sat beside him gloomily, pulling at his ears.

"Now he's left. She'll be miserable for days," Magda whispered, nodding her head in Marian's direction.

"Shall I follow and track him down?" John asked.

Marian shook her head. "It will take time for us all to struggle through this disaster."

Brother James came and settled himself beside the two girls. "Now the lads are mending, let's have a look at this dog of yours." He gently pressed his fingers into Fetcher's mutilated paw while Joanna watched anxiously. "It's healing well," he murmured.

"Will he walk again, do you think?"

"Oh aye, he'll walk. He'll do more than that, with the right training. He'll make as fine a bodyguard as any lass could want."

"Would you help me, sir?" Joanna begged.

Brother James smiled. "Certainly I will. We'll have him lolloping about in no time."

In the weeks that followed, Brother James set to training Fetcher as though his life depended on it. Each day he went out into the woods with the two girls, tempting the dog onto his feet with meat scraps, till at last Fetcher could run from one to the other with a strange, lopsided gait. His muscles grew hard and strong, his coat glossy, and they progressed to slinging bones and straw-stuffed sacks for him to fetch.

John stayed in the clearing, and Magda was pleased to have her father by her side.

On a hot afternoon toward the end of August they were lazily sitting in the sun outside the hut when they heard the sound of hooves. As always they sprang to their feet and melted into the lower branches of the yew trees.

"One horse," whispered John, "though a big 'un, I'd guess. Seems to stamp four times, then stops." Suddenly John was laughing. "Tom! That's his signal, though I've never heard it done on horseback."

They came out from their hiding places, wondering how Tom had got himself a horse. There was only a moment to wait before he came trotting into the clearing astride a fine gray stallion.

"I have the oil!" he shouted. "I have the oil and more besides!"

"Well!" John laughed. "At least one of us has done summat right."

Everyone cheered and gathered around, patting the horse and touching its good halter and bridle with amazement.

"Good quality gear, is this," said Brother James. "The best."

"You've taken so long," Magda cried. "I thought you were dead in some ditch."

"Not me." Tom laughed, sliding down from the saddle and kissing her cheek. "Walter of Stainthorpe was not with the Templars at Newhouse. I had to travel on to the wastes of Bitterwood."

"Where's this marvelous oil?" Marian asked.

Tom patted a strong leather pouch fastened to his waist.

He ate and drank with them, and was saddened to hear of Much. But despite this he was eager to be off to the Magdalen convent with his precious oil. "I've much to tell Mother Veronica," he said. "I've done myself a lot of good, but I've sorry news for her."

"Oh dear," said Brother James. "Shall I come with you? Is her man dead?"

"No," said Tom. "Not dead, but maybe he wishes he was. He's taken the leprosy himself. He grows aged and weak, and his face is fearfully marked. He came back from Outremer with the seeds of sickness in him. That's why he was not at Temple Newhouse. He's gone to live in a wild and lonely place with five other fighting monks, all suffering like himself."

"Now then," Brother James sighed. "I believe I have heard of some such men. Do they call themselves the Knights of Saint Lazarus?"

"That's it," said Tom. "They still endeavor to live by the Templars' strict rules. They pray and keep their fighting skills sharp, but they live in the wilderness as outcast as we."

"As hard a life as ours, and worse," John agreed.

"But Walter of Stainthorpe has given me this fine gray stallion," exclaimed Tom. "He's grown too old and weak to manage such a spirited steed, and their rule states that they must give away all they cannot use. The knight has found himself a quieter mount, and Rambler is mine!"

They all admired the powerful beast.

"Can you manage him?" asked John with a touch of envy.

"Certainly I can. He's trained to obey every small command. Didn't you hear? I can get him to stamp out my signal!"

John laughed and slapped the horse's rump. Tom galloped off to visit the convent, returning in the morning still pleased with himself.

Weeks went by and there was no word from Robert.

As autumn approached, Marian made them all set about the yearly gathering. Everything possible must be garnered from the woods and stored before the first frosts. Nuts, berries, mushrooms, ladies' bedstraw, and meadowsweet all had their uses; dried poppy heads, hard-skinned sloes, and sour-tasting juniper berries were carefully collected and carried back to the clearing. The work was a little less arduous this year, as John, Tom, and Brother James all stayed to help. No message or sign came from Robert.

Fetcher's training went better than ever, and though he still limped, Brother James taught him a few good tricks. He could snatch away a weapon with one fast snap of his jaws, disarming a man before he knew what came at him. And catching flying arrows in his mouth was Fetcher's favorite sport.

October was the pannage month, when pigs were herded into the woods to search for acorns. One afternoon, Marian stirred dark red elderberries in a tub of dye, while Tom and Fetcher brought sticks for Joanna and Magda's charcoal stack. John and Brother James sat by the doorsill in the sharp autumn sun.

Marian turned to them. "That lass and her dog should be returned home," she said. "Somehow we've forgotten, what with all the trouble and hurts. I daresay she thinks she belongs here, but she should be back with her parents before winter comes."

John nodded and scratched his beard. "Shall we take her home?" he asked Brother James.

The monk nodded. "We grow too safe and fat sitting here," he agreed. "A little outing to Clipstone would do us fine."

"Take her now, while the pannage lasts," said Marian. "Traveling will be at its safest, with the woods full of pigs and children."

Though Magda cried when they left, Marian insisted. "Her parents will have given up hope," she said, and Joanna agreed that she could not leave them in distress. She hugged Magda fiercely.

"One day I'll come back," she said.

16

Bad News
Travels Fast

THE MEN WERE GONE for four days, but then they came hurrying back into the clearing with glum faces and the dog still at their heels.

"Father, why have you brought Fetcher back?" Magda demanded.

"He would not leave James's side," John told her hurriedly. "But we have more to bother us than Fetcher, sweetheart."

Marian put down the pot she pounded roots in. "What is it now?" she demanded.

"The king has been at Clipstone hunting lodge with the sheriff."

"What of that? He hunts while the weather's warm."

John shook his head. "He's gone on to Nottingham now, but he's left the sheriff and that damned FitzRanulf at Clipstone. There's the remains of the wolf pack and, with them, a great gang of new mercenaries."

A shiver crept up Magda's back when she heard her father's words.

"We don't like the look of it." Brother James's face was grim. "That's no jolly hunting party gathering there—they've got three blacksmiths hard at work preparing their weapons.

We did not hang around to be recognized. We came at close quarters to some of them, up at Wentbridge."

Marian frowned and looked around at her mother. "Is this it?" she asked. "Is this the great fear that haunts your dreams?"

Eleanor had gone very white. "I think so," she whispered.

Magda dug her fingers deep into Fetcher's warm, rough coat for comfort.

"What do they plan? Can you tell us, old one?" Brother James begged, but Eleanor shook her head.

"Fire and sword," she said. "Fire, sword, and hunger in the forest . . . nay, in Langden. I cannot see more."

"Damn it! I wish that Robert was here," John said. "Should I go off hunting for him?"

"Aye, maybe the time is right that you should," Marian agreed.

The following morning John set out to track his friend down. Tom and Brother James went snaring hares for the pot, and those left in the clearing went about their tasks with an air of foreboding. Their fears were heightened when Philippa arrived, breathless and angry, just before midday.

"What is it?" Marian cried, running to her friend. "Bad news?"

"Aye," Philippa gasped. "Bad news for Langden. It's the wolf pack, all the lot of them. They've marched in and taken over the manor house. They're bristling with weapons and foulmouthed as sin."

"What of Isabel and Matilda? Have they been turned out?"

"Nay. Not so bad if they had. At least we could give them shelter then. No one has seen them—the wolf pack will let nobody in or out."

"What does it mean?" Marian demanded.

Magda's heart thumped fast as she watched the two women striding up and down the clearing. They were unaware of the goats, chickens, and cats who scattered in their path, so deep was their concern. Magda's safe existence in Barnsdale seemed badly threatened. The old one watched anxiously from the doorsill.

When Tom and Brother James returned with a pair of hares, they all sat down and talked again.

"What can we do against so many?"

"There's no way that we can raise more men, not after our last defeat!"

Brother James shook his head despairingly. Then suddenly he got up. "One thing I do know: I'd rather die than cower here in the woods."

"Me too," agreed Marian. "But what shall we do?"

Brother James shrugged his shoulders. "Bow practice," he said. "Come on, every one of us. Don't sit here worrying; let's string our bows and be ready to make our move when we may."

They all jumped up at his suggestion. Anything was better than sitting there in gloom. They worked all afternoon, fitting new shafts for their arrows. They were grimly letting the arrows fly at a swaying willow wand when Sister Rosamund came tramping through the woods with worse news.

"It's Mother Veronica," she told them. "She went visiting the Langden ladies yesterday and she's not returned. I've been to the manor to ask after her, but there's soldiers at every door and they won't let me in. The little windows up in Matilda's solar are boarded up, though I thought I could hear a scraping sound from within. I fear they've all been taken prisoner."

"This gets worse and worse," Marian cried.

"I must go to Langden," Brother James insisted.

Tom looked thoughtful. "No, wait awhile." he said. "They may have made a great mistake when they imprisoned Mother Veronica. Walter of Stainthorpe may be old and sick, but he still leads a band of fierce fighting men."

Brother James looked suddenly interested. "You mean the leper knights? They're not exactly an army, but you are right, Tom; they're trained as sharp as any fighting men and fiercely disciplined. I've heard it said that once they move to fight they will never turn back, even though they face certain death."

"But would such men give us aid?" asked Marian.

"I believe so," said Tom. "Though both devoted their lives to God, Walter of Stainthorpe is still Mother Veronica's man and would do anything for her."

Philippa was puzzled by mention of the leper knights, but Marian was eager now. "What have we to lose?"

Tom led out Rambler, the stallion, from the lean-to where they'd stabled him and climbed into the saddle. "Come on, fellow," he murmured. "I bet you never thought to see your old master so soon."

Magda could not stop herself from running to Tom and grabbing his leg. "Take care!" she implored. "Please come safely back! We are all depending on you!"

Tom looked surprised but pleased and stooped from the saddle to kiss her. "I'll be back as fast as you can blink," he promised.

The ones that were left sat whispering together around the fire that night, then slept badly once they had settled to rest. Two more days passed in constant fear and anxiety. Plans were made, only to be discarded as hopeless and ridiculous. Then early on the fourth day after news of the Langden ladies' imprisonment had reached the clearing, Marian and the others were surprised by the sound of voices calling out their names.

Magda lifted up the curtain of skins and stepped over the doorsill, thinking that she recognized one of the voices. And she was right. Joanna stood before her with an older man and a lad.

Magda went to hug her, filled with surprise. "What's brought you back so soon?"

"We've walked all through the night, me and Father and Jamie, for Jamie has heard some terrible things that we think you should know."

Marian came up behind Magda, also amazed to see Joanna back again. "What is it?" she asked.

"Our Jamie is apprenticed to Clipstone's blacksmith," Joanna told them. "And while he was stoking the fires he heard two soldiers from the wolf pack boasting of what they did. He didn't like the sound of it. You tell them, Jamie!"

Everyone gathered around the doorway, looking expectantly at the young lad.

"They said," he muttered nervously, "they said that Matilda and Isabel of Langden were to get the same as the great Matilda."

"You know who they mean," Joanna wailed. "That brave lady, the one you tried to rescue."

"Yes," Marian agreed. "We do fear greatly that the wolf pack has imprisoned Langden's ladies in their own home, along with Mother Veronica. And that is what we suppose has happened to the great Matilda de Braose."

" 'Tis worse than that," Joanna cried. "Go on, Jamie! Tell them what else you heard."

"Well," said Jamie hesitantly, "I can't be certain that I understood their meaning right, but they said that the great Matilda and her son have gone without their dinner, and Langden's ladies shall do the same!"

They all frowned at that, unsure what it might mean.

Then Jamie spoke up again. "They began laughing in the most horrible way and . . . I'm not sure, but I fear the worst. . . ."

The whole company stood horrified as his thought sank in.

"Can it really mean . . . they would starve them?" Philippa cried. "Imprison them and starve them to death?"

Suddenly the old one was shaking; her eyes ran with tears. "Yes, they would," she whispered. "This is it! This is my dream. I have no doubt. Sword and fire and hunger!"

←≡17≡→

STEALTH INSTEAD
OF STRENGTH

A DREADFUL SILENCE followed, so that the bleating of goats and soft clucking of fowls was all that could be heard. Then Marian whispered, "No. No, surely. They have Mother Veronica there too. They would not dare to starve a nun!"

Brother James laughed bitterly at that. "Would they not? Since the king still quarrels with the pope, the church gets no protection at all. I heard just last month that a party of nuns was stoned outside Nottingham. The sheriff's men stood by giving encouragement. Indeed, King John would probably pay his mercenaries double for ridding him of a troublesome nun as well as two defiant women."

"The wolf pack would do anything," said Philippa with certainty. "You cannot believe the foulness of their mood. I fear they do not forget the outlaws' attack at Wentbridge."

"But they don't know that Matilda and Isabel have anything to do with us," said Magda. "Do they?"

Brother James shrugged his shoulders. "They'd pay well for such information, and if the king is in a temper, anyone can come off the worse. There is no fairness or sense about it."

There was another moment of quiet while they thought, then Marian's hand went slowly to the meat knife that she always carried tucked into her belt.

"We must do something," she said. "Anything. We cannot wait for Tom or John or Robert, or leper knights who may never come."

"Yes," Brother James agreed. "But we must not go rushing up there without any kind of plan; they'd kill us quick as a flash. No . . . we must work out the best way to use our small strength."

"That's right," Philippa agreed. "How many have we got on our side to start with?"

Brother James patted her shoulder. "You've a fat monk who's handy with a quarterstaff and a well-trained dog." Then he turned to Marian. "You've a woman who's fast with a knife and a fine archer."

"Two," shouted Magda. "I am as good a shot as any."

Marian looked unhappy at that, but Philippa nodded her head. "We need every scrap of help we can gather," she said. "All who live at Langden will support us, though they've few weapons or fighting skills, and we have a convent full of angry nuns."

They smiled at that thought, but then Philippa shook her head at Marian. "It's you that should not come. The Forestwife should not leave Barnsdale Forest."

Marian folded her arms stubbornly. "I'll not be left behind."

"I can help," said Eleanor, and she pointed to Marian's beautiful woven girdle, the symbol of her work as Forestwife. "Take it off, Daughter!" she said. "Give it to me. There shall be a Forestwife here for those in need, however long you are gone and whatever becomes of you. I will use my small skills and do the best I can."

Marian did not hesitate. "Thank you, Mother," she said, unfastening the belt and giving it to the old one with a kiss.

"Now," said Brother James, "we must make our plans and act together. We need stealth instead of strength. In place of swords we'll carry food and water flasks, as we fear starvation. In place of sling stones, we'll carry wood and kindling and tinder, for they may need warmth."

Most looked puzzled at that, but Marian picked up the way his mind worked. "Aye," she said. "I like your way of thinking, Brother James. Instead of lances and pikes, we shall need hammers, chisels, and nails. For we must get inside with the prisoners and barricade ourselves in with them."

Brother James nodded. "I fear we must settle for a siege!"

"Ah, Brother James," Marian said, her eyes glittering. "I have a wicked idea. Use what strengths we've got, you said. I've been drying my special herbs for many years—now I know what I saved them for." She went into the cottage and carefully reached up to the high shelf, bringing down an earthenware pot.

Magda caught her breath. "The forbidden herbs," she whispered.

Marian's smile made her shiver. "That's right, child. A healer can turn poisoner, easy as that," and she snapped her fingers. "What did Robert tell you? Death shall not be good enough for FitzRanulf. Now I begin to see how."

Magda had never seen Marian so determined. She rushed about the clearing giving orders and instructions. Her furious energy raised their spirits and catapulted them into action. For Magda, though, the change in Marian brought a touch of fear. She could not believe this was the calm, steadfast woman who'd mothered her so long.

By dusk they'd made themselves ready and packed their weapons and bags. Magda was exhausted from running backward and forward through the forest tracks carrying messages to the nuns and to Langden forge.

They tried to settle to sleep, but it was difficult. Each time Magda opened her eyes, she saw the dark shape of Marian still moving about.

Before dawn Marian woke them all and handed out rushlights. "The time has come," she whispered. They obeyed without a sound.

They reached the outskirts of Langden before the sun rose, Marian and Magda with bows and quivers strapped to their backs, along with sacks of bread, cheese and grain. Magda looked anxiously up at the dark shape of Langden Manor on its low mound. The ditch that surrounded the thatched stone-built house, with its courtyard and barns, had only a trickle of water in it. The low stockade around the garden was just high enough to keep in pigs and fowl. Magda remembered the great stone turrets of Nottingham Castle; beside it Langden seemed so homely.

"What does FitzRanulf want with marrying Isabel?" she asked. "Langden's nowt but barns and kitchen gardens."

"He doesn't really want Isabel," Marian told her. "He wants the land. I daresay he has plans to tear down this old house and build a grand hunting lodge in its place."

"How can he treat her so badly, if he hopes to marry her?"

Marian looked grim. "I fear this is punishment for refusal. He does not care whether Isabel lives or dies."

They crept past the church and met Philippa's husband behind the forge.

"Why must we be stumbling about so early in the dark?" Magda asked.

"To catch them unawares," Philippa told her. "They have

their weaknesses. They are all drunken sots and will be snoring in their straw."

It was not long before Magda turned and saw faint lights moving deep in the woods. "Here comes our diversion," she whispered to Marian.

As the lights came nearer, they smelled the smoky scent of incense and saw a solemn, chanting procession winding its way toward Langden. Each light was carried by one of the Magdalen nuns. Sister Rosamund was in front, Alan at her side.

"Time for me to join them," said Brother James. "I'll go to rally help as soon as I know that you are inside."

He kissed Marian and the others solemnly and then went to head the procession with Sister Rosamund and Joanna's family. The three women with their bows watched from behind the forge as Philippa's husband strode from hut to hut, whispering low. The villagers came quietly from their hovels to swell the ranks of the strange procession. The singing grew louder, and some of the wolf pack who'd been sleeping out in the courtyard leapt, puzzled, to their feet. They pulled out their swords and started shouting at one another.

Brother James marched up to the open outer gate. "We demand to see Lady Matilda!" he bellowed.

"We must speak with our prioress," cried Sister Rosamund.

FitzRanulf himself came yawning from the hall with straw in his hair. He drew his sword and thrust it toward Brother James's throat.

"Who dares to ask?" he growled.

Magda caught her breath in fear, but Marian whispered, "Trust in Brother James! Now's our moment."

Though her legs shook and her stomach heaved, Magda clutched her bow tightly and followed Marian and Philippa as they ran quietly around the stockade and in at the small back gate to the kitchen gardens. They jumped the ditch and crept past the grunting pigs, past Isabel's neat rows of beans and onions, making for the kitchen door. They paused for a moment, not knowing what they would find on the other side.

" 'Tis now or never," Philippa hissed.

Marian turned to Magda. "Brave lass," she whispered. "Are you ready?"

"Aye." Magda nodded.

Philippa tried the heavy wooden latch and gave a good push, almost falling in as the door swung open. A frightened kitchen maid turned to see them.

"Don't fear, Margery," Philippa whispered. " 'Tis us, come to help. Where are Matilda and Isabel?"

Margery pointed up the narrow stairs to the solar and burst into tears.

"Are they locked in?" Marian asked.

" 'Tis worse, far worse." Margery swallowed hard, and tears spilled down her cheeks.

Marian pulled her bundles of herbs from her pack and pushed them into Margery's hand. "Here—put this in their food or drink; this first and then the other. Only the wolf pack, mind—only them!"

Margery took the bundles with shaking hands as the three intruders dashed up the narrow wooden stairs.

Philippa pulled back a rich tapestry curtain that covered the doorway and stared at the solid, blank stones that formed a new-made wall. "Dear God!" she cried. "It's true."

──❦18❦──

WATER HAS NEVER
TASTED SO SWEET

THE CLATTER OF swords and heavy boots came from
below, then men's voices bellowing in a foreign tongue.
Marian slipped her bow from her back and notched an
arrow, covering the narrow way up the stairs. Philippa pulled
hammer and chisel from her bag and set to work to loosen
the stones. "If we could shift just one," she said, "then the
others would come easy."

Magda pulled the meat knife from Marian's belt and
began to work at the stone with Philippa. A grumpy, yawning
soldier appeared at the bottom of the stairs.

"Stupid hags," he snarled, lunging toward Marian with
his sword. He soon fell back, cursing, as Marian's arrow
pierced his hand. His sword clattered to the floor, and fast
as a whip she notched another arrow. She let fly again,
wounding a second fellow in the shoulder. Much cursing
followed, then sudden quiet.

FitzRanulf appeared at the bottom of the stairs, furious
that he'd been rushed back into the house when he was trying
to deal with the strange deputation of nuns and villagers.
"Damned fools!" he bellowed at his men.

"There's three ragged forest women up there!"

"The hellcats—they've split my thumb!"

"They're raining down arrows like needles! We can't reach up to spit them."

"So what?" FitzRanulf gave a chilling laugh. "Where do you think they are going? Now we have six witches to starve instead of three. Just guard the stairs, damn you, and don't let any of them down."

Philippa sighed, then grunted with effort. "It gives!"

Marian turned to Magda. "Can you cover the stairs?"

"Aye."

The two older women worked at the stone with their chisels and knives, and at last a definite grating movement rewarded them. Magda stood at the top of the stairs with arrow notched and bow bent. It was very uncomfortable; the sharp straw of the thatch came down low and stuck into her head. Her arms ached with the tension of the ready bow. One of the men looked up again through the narrow stairwell.

"I see nothing but a stupid child," he sneered.

"But I can shoot," Magda answered, and loosed an arrow that landed with a *thwack* in the wooden beam just by his ear. The fellow withdrew fast, swearing furiously, though Magda could not understand the words he used. Her hands shook and she felt sick, but she whipped out another arrow.

"It's sliding away," Philippa hissed. "Push, push . . . someone is helping from the other side."

Then with one great heave, the stone slithered away and landed with a thump.

"Help us! Oh, help us!" a faint voice cried.

Philippa opened her tinderbox and struck the flint sharply while Marian held a rushlight to pick up the tiny flames. As soon as it was burning steadily, they thrust the small wand into the hole. It was snatched at by bloodstained fingers with ripped, dirty nails. Then they saw the shadowy top of Isabel's head, covered in dust.

"Water! Water, for the love of God!" Isabel choked out the words.

Marian pulled a small water skin from her belt.

"Quick! Quick!" Isabel sobbed. "Mother Veronica will not leave Mother's side. I fear she is dying."

"Hush, sweetheart," soothed Marian. "We have good food and drink with us."

Isabel's poor torn hands came stretching through the gap. Greedy fingers closed about the water skin and vanished.

"Listen, Isabel." Marian put her mouth to the dusty hole. "You must give them just a small sip each, then wait awhile, or they'll die for sure with bloated stomachs."

"Yes." Her voice floated back to them. "I understand."

"Are they strong enough to hold back, do you think?" Philippa asked anxiously.

"We are," came a sharp reply.

"That was Mother Veronica." Philippa smiled to hear her voice so firm.

They set about moving more stones with renewed energy. They worked steadily, and soon Isabel came back to help from the other side.

"Bless you! Bless you!" she murmured. "Water has never tasted so sweet."

They worked on, and Isabel tore at the stones from her side. At last, without turning, Marian spoke to Magda. "Are you still taking aim, my brave lass?"

"Aye," she answered through gritted teeth. "But I can't keep it up much longer!"

"I think you can let up," said Philippa. "This is wide enough for a little 'un, and that's you, my girl."

"Come, Magda," said Marian. "Climb through this hole, and I shall take your place again!"

Magda lowered her aim and waggled her aching shoulders with relief. Marian snatched up the bow.

"I'll heave," said Philippa, bending to cup her hands like a stirrup.

Magda stuck her head through the hole into the shadowy room. "It smells bad in here," she said.

"Aye, love, it will," Philippa told her. "Murder always smells foul. But don't be afraid. 'Tis only the odors of our friends' poor bodies, struggling to stay alive."

Isabel took hold of Magda's shoulders to pull her through. They both fell into the darkness together, and it was only when Mother Veronica came over with the rushlight that Magda saw the terrible state of Isabel. Exhaustion was clear on her thin, dusty face; her clothes were torn, her feet and fingers bleeding.

"Oh, Isabel," Magda cried with pity, hugging her tight.

"Bless you," Isabel sobbed. "I could not see how anyone could help us."

"I'm not so sure that we are such a wonderful help." Philippa's down-to-earth tones came to them through the hole. "I fear we've come to share this cruel imprisonment with you."

Bread and goat's milk were handed through the hole. "Just a small sop each," Marian warned.

Magda tore the fresh bread into tiny pieces and dribbled the milk onto them in her cupped hand. She'd fed folk close to starvation before, though never had she cared so much that they should be revived. When all three had taken their small portion of food, Magda and Isabel set about working more stones loose, and at last the hole was big enough for Philippa and Marian to scramble through.

"But can't they come up here and get us now?" Magda cried.

"Quick," Marian told her. "Fit these stones back into the wall. Their cruel intentions will provide us with some safety, at least for a little while."

Once the hole was filled again, they began to take stock of their situation.

Marian took a small ax from her pack. "At least we can get a bit more daylight in here." She began to hack at the shutters.

"They nailed them up and left us with nothing," Isabel told them. "They took Mother's bed for FitzRanulf and did not even leave us straw."

When at last the morning light came through the windows, Philippa and Magda crammed together to look down at the gateway. Brother James and the nuns still stood their ground, though FitzRanulf had his men arrayed against them, swords drawn.

"Leave now," FitzRanulf bellowed. "This moment. The sheriff will soon be at Langden. All those who do not leave shall be arrested. We serve the king."

"Time for our signal," said Philippa.

"Aye." Marian caught up her bow and took careful aim from the window.

"Leave now," FitzRanulf barked again. He snatched hold of Sister Rosamund roughly, hauling her away from Brother James. "I'll start with this sweet-faced nun."

At that moment Marian loosed her arrow; it fell with a thud before FitzRanulf's feet, startling the man.

Brother James held up his hand as though he submitted. "We will go," he said. "We want no trouble from the sheriff."

The nuns and villagers stepped back from the gate, but Brother James stubbornly held out his hand for Rosamund.

FitzRanulf released her with a shove. "The king thinks poorly of meddling nuns," he growled. "He's still got bishops who will bring a charge of heresy. We like the smell of burning nuns—remember that!"

The three women at the window watched as their friends melted away into the village and woods. When at last they had gone, the women sat down wearily.

"What now?" Magda asked.

⟨19⟩

A LOT OF MEN
TO FEED

THERE WAS SILENCE in the dark, bare solar, then Philippa spoke up with her usual common sense. "What now? We wait," she said. "We trust in Brother James and set about making ourselves as comfortable and safe as we may. We must work out our rations; fresh food first, and then the grain."

"It's lack of water that I fear most," said Isabel.

Philippa put out three large water skins and the food they'd brought. "We must sip carefully and eke it out as best we can."

"If we're very careful, we might last a sennight," said Marian.

"Can there be any help for us?" Isabel asked.

Marian nodded. "Our friends will not desert us." She told how John had gone off to find Robert and that Brother James would rally all the aid he could get.

"Tom has gone to find your Templar knight," Magda told Mother Veronica.

"What, sweetheart?" The old nun looked startled for a moment.

" 'Tis true," Magda assured her. "Do you think he'll come?"

Mother Veronica returned to her usual calm. "I cannot say. From what Tom tells me, he is sick and terribly marked, but . . . ," she added a little wistfully, "he was always a brave man and did what he believed right."

It was clear that Isabel and Mother Veronica desperately needed rest, and Matilda careful feeding. Marian suggested that she and Philippa act as lookout and nurse while the others slept.

Magda was trying to get comfortable beneath her cloak when it dawned on her that sleep was not at all what her body required. She rolled over and got up. "You sleep, Marian," she said firmly. "I will watch Lady Matilda; I know what to do. You did not sleep at all last night."

Marian opened her mouth to argue, but somehow the calm sense of Magda's words made her close it again. Instead she kissed her and obeyed, falling quickly into a deep sleep of exhaustion.

While she slept, Philippa and Magda tucked their cloaks around Matilda and set a small fire burning on the hearthstone. They cleaned the solar and tidied their food and tools.

Marian woke with a start. "How long have I slept?" she demanded. "What has happened? What have they done?"

"Hush!" Philippa told her. "They have ventured up the staircase, and I believe they've set a guard out there, but naught else. Why should they do more? They've got us where they want us, haven't they? They do not know we've friends. They think they may sit tight and let us die without raising a weapon."

"Do you think that's what's happened to Matilda de Braose?" Magda asked.

Philippa and Marian looked grimly at each other and nodded their heads.

"And her son too?"

Marian sighed. "I fear so."

"If my father knew that I was here, he'd come raging through the gates at them," said Magda. "He'd get himself killed."

Marian smiled and nodded. "But Robert is a wicked crafty fellow," she said. "He'll have other plans, and he and Brother James will hold John back."

"And what of Tom?"

"Who knows," said Marian.

Three days passed, and they took turns at keeping watch at the window. Lady Matilda gained strength from the careful feeding, but Magda was hungry. The bread and cheese and milk were gone, their kindling turned to ashes. Now they had to crush the grain and mix the meal with a trickle of water to make a cold, sticky porridge that did not satisfy.

"We must keep ourselves strong," Marian insisted. "We must be ready to run or fight."

She made them bend and stretch in the confined space and practice drawing bows, though they did not let their arrows fly. Even poor weak Matilda had to flex her fingers and toes and allow the others to rub her stiff shoulders and spine. Isabel was greatly cheered by their company and the hope they brought.

It was on the third day that the sound of horses arriving brought them to the window. Magda recognized the sheriff, at the head of a band of men just as heavily armed as the wolf pack. FitzRanulf went out to meet him, and it was clear from the way they looked up toward the solar windows that the women's fate was being discussed, though Marian and the others could not hear what was said.

Magda shivered at the sight of them crowding into the

courtyard. "So many men and weapons," she murmured.

Marian put an arm around her shoulders and hugged her tight. "But remember, love, we do not only fight with weapons. We have different ways of doing things."

They watched as the men pitched camp—some inside the house, others outside. Some of the kitchen servants lit a fire and set up a cooking pot out in the courtyard.

"It's a lot of men to be fed," Magda said resentfully. "And whatever they get to eat, they'll be better fed than me."

Marian smiled. "Maybe not," she whispered. "I doubt the kitchen servants will relish this extra work. See who stirs broth for the wolfhounds?"

Magda glanced down, her mouth watering at the good smell that rose from the pot. "Why, it's Margery."

"Aye." Marian nodded. "Do you trust the lass?" she asked Isabel.

"Yes." Isabel was definite. "She's a bold one, and I'd trust her with my life."

Late that evening, when the soldiers had eaten and drunk, Magda was surprised to hear the sounds of quiet laughter. It was Marian, chuckling as she stood at her watch place by the window.

"What is it?" Magda asked, going to her side.

"Brave Margery!" she said with relish. "Listen!"

"It sounds like someone being sick," said Magda, puzzled.

"It's lots of people being sick," Marian told her. "You see, love, they did not get better food than we."

Magda understood. "The forbidden herbs!"

"Yes," said Marian. "Some are deadly, some are not. Margery has done her task well."

The sounds of choking and retching came from the ditch

at the side of the manor house. The women in the solar could see the pale shapes of running men, dropping their breeches to the ground as they dashed outside to squat wherever they might.

Magda and the others crowded at the window, stifling their laughter. Philippa put her hand over Mother Veronica's eyes. "This is not a sight any nun should see," she chuckled.

Mother Veronica laughed till the tears rolled down her cheeks. "God bless Margery," she said.

"Oh yes," said Marian. "She's done very well."

"Will the fellows die?"

Marian shook her head. "No. They'll be weak and weary for a few days, but they'll not die from a good clear-out. Still, Margery has other herbs than those in her care."

One of the soldiers looked up at their narrow window and shook his fist. "Barnsdale's witch!" he shouted. "We're cursed!"

20

THE BEST RIGHT
OF ALL

THE FOLLOWING DAY there was an outbreak of spots and rashes among the mercenaries. The women watched from the windows as men scratched themselves against walls and fences, some rolling on the ground. Despite their own hunger, the sights below brought hope.

But again the soldiers gathered in groups in the courtyard, pointing up to the window and making signs against the evil eye. "Barnsdale's witch! Barnsdale's witch!" they chanted. "She should burn!"

"I don't like it," Magda whispered.

"Better they think it's my curse than Margery's stew pot," said Marian.

They sat huddled together that evening, watching their last scrap of candle burn.

"It must soon be All Hallows' Eve," Magda said, sighing. "Oh, how I long for soul cake and costumes and crackling bonfires."

"Why, yes," Mother Veronica agreed. "It must be soon. Can we have missed it?"

"You've not missed it," Marian told them. "It's All Hallows' Eve tonight."

"Oh no," Mother Veronica cried. "I've been so muddled,

I've lost track." She bowed her head and started to murmur the special prayers for the dead.

Marian took Magda's hand. "Don't worry," she said. "This little candle is our All Hallows fire. We'll wish upon it, and whisper all our hopes for the coming year."

Next day their hopes looked bleak, for the sheriff and FitzRanulf marched out into the courtyard when the sun was high in the sky. "Now!" they growled. "Bring the slut out here so that her friends may see!"

"Oh no!" whispered Isabel. The women crowded at the windows.

Two men dragged Margery out between them.

"How do they know?" Magda cried. "What will they do?"

They watched in helpless silence as the men tied Margery to a post.

The wolf pack gathered, pale and wretched after a sleepless night. Some clutched their stomachs, others still scratched; all were very angry. "Poisoner!" they shouted. "Stone her! Stone her!"

Marian quickly picked up her bow and took aim from the window.

Magda watched with horror. "How can we save her, against so many?"

Marian shook her head desperately. "We can't, but we can see she does not die alone."

"Aye," Magda agreed, and snatched up her own bow.

The wolf pack set about collecting stones and dung from the yard, filling the air with foul threats.

"Look . . . look!" Marian cried, sudden hope in her voice.

From their viewpoint high above the courtyard, they could see that a lone rider had emerged from behind Langden Church, cantering slowly toward the manor. The man wore fine chain mail and the white tunic of a Templar knight. His shield was emblazoned with a red cross, but his face was hidden by a huge white linen hood.

FitzRanulf stared openmouthed as the knight in full battle dress reached the manor, dipping his head to enter through the outer gate.

"Who the hell . . . ?" the sheriff shouted.

"Saint Lazarus," FitzRanulf muttered, backing away. "Leper knight—beware!"

The knight of Saint Lazarus brought his horse to a standstill behind Margery. His face was bandaged inside the hood, so that only his eyes could be seen. He raised his hand and spoke in a cracked and muffled voice, though he could be heard well enough in the shocked silence. "Let the women go!"

The sheriff and FitzRanulf looked at each other.

"What interest has the Temple in old women and witches?" the sheriff asked. "Here, help us burn the lot of them!"

The Templar drew his sword. "Let them go!" he repeated.

Magda turned to Mother Veronica. "Is it your man?" she whispered.

Silent tears poured down Mother Veronica's cheeks. "Aye, I believe it is he."

"But what can he do, one man alone?" Magda asked.

Marian touched her shoulder and pointed. "Not alone—not alone at all."

Magda looked where she was bidden, out toward Langden village, and there she saw another Saint Lazarus knight riding out from behind the huts. His tunic was black with a red cross on the chest, and a black hood shaded his face.

"See there," hissed Philippa.

Yet another hooded knight in black came from behind

the forge; a broad-built fellow, this one. Beside his horse bounded a limping dog.

"Fetcher!" Magda cried with delight. "And see that horse behind . . . I know it. It's Rambler! But where is Tom? Who are these knights?"

"They are the costumes you wished for!" Marian's face was full of joy.

They watched then as more appeared, until a company of ten leper knights came cantering slowly and silently toward the manor house.

The sheriff was pop-eyed with astonishment. Slowly a huge multitude gathered behind the Templars. They came flooding out from the quiet huts of Langden: villagers carrying forks and sickles, coal diggers with spades, and charcoal burners with great quarterstaffs.

The women laughed out loud as the numbers grew.

"Where have so many come from?" Isabel cried. "They are not all our people!"

Mother Veronica stood beside her frowning, then she suddenly snorted with laughter. "That's no villager," she exclaimed. "That's Sister Rosamund in lad's breeches!"

FitzRanulf swung around frantically as the ten leper knights headed steadily toward the low stockade. He turned to his men in panic. "Fools!" he shouted. "To your weapons!"

All hell was let loose as the men dropped their stones and snatched up swords and lances. FitzRanulf pulled a blazing brand from the cooking fire and threw it into the open doorway of the house. "At least the witch shall burn!" he cried.

Then Magda watched, appalled, as FitzRanulf raised his sword—not to one of the advancing fighting men, but to poor helpless Margery. Without stopping to think, she bent her bow and aimed between his shoulders. Her arrow sang through the air and buried itself deep in his back.

FitzRanulf staggered, then turned toward the house, a ridiculous expression of surprise written clear on his face. His sword clattered uselessly onto the ground at Margery's feet as he crumpled and fell, disappearing amid the dust and fighting that now surrounded him.

Utter chaos reigned. Some of the mercenaries made a good fight of it, but most ran off into the woods, still sick and fearful, clutching their stomachs. The leper knights fought bitterly, and Marian rained down arrows from the window, taking careful aim and making sure she hit the right targets.

Magda could not stop trembling; tears poured down her face. "I have killed a man," she whispered to Mother Veronica.

The old woman gently took away the bow and hugged her tightly. "You have saved Margery," she said.

The Knights of Saint Lazarus, supported by the villagers, soon found themselves in charge of the courtyard. One black-hooded knight bent quickly to untie Margery. She wrapped her arms about his neck and clung to him. The man flung back his hood, and the women cheered to see Robert's scarred, excited face. The big man beside him ripped back his hood, and Magda saw that it was her father. Behind him came Brother James, and beside him on Rambler was Tom. But the bandaged knight with the husky voice did not remove his hood, nor did five more who gathered beside him.

There was no time for rejoicing, for thick black smoke began to billow out from the hall. The men saw the danger and looked about desperately for help.

"No water!" Robert bellowed. "Can't save the house!"

"Just get them out!" John roared.

Robert leapt from his horse and ran to Isabel's low wooden stockade. "John! John!" he cried, starting to tear up the wooden fencing.

John understood and went to help. Soon all the villagers were tearing up the low fence of palings. They carried it to the manor house and propped it up beneath the window.

One by one, all the women except for Marian climbed out precariously onto the rough wooden fencing. They slithered down it, picking up grazes and splinters, but they did not feel them much or even care. Getting Lady Matilda out was more awkward, but the villagers brought ropes and, as the flames of her home crackled behind her, Marian safely lowered the old lady to the ground, then quickly clambered down herself.

Robert snatched up Marian and swung her around until she shouted at him to stop. Magda flung her arms around Tom.

Mother Veronica walked boldly toward the six leper knights. Walter of Stainthorpe held up his gloved hand to halt her. She stopped obediently by his horse's head. Tears filled her eyes as she bent to kiss his stirrup.

Magda saw her father stamping out flames on the wooden fencing. She ran to him, but stumbled and fell over Fitz-Ranulf's body. John bent at once to help his daughter to her feet, glaring down at the remains of his enemy. Fitz-Ranulf's white, dead face still carried that surprised expression.

"Evil man!" John spat. "I should have been the one to kill him, not Marian."

Marian turned as she heard his words. "I did not fire that shot from my bow," she said.

"Who then?" John cried.

"The one who had the best right of us all," she told him, gently touching Magda's shoulder.

John turned to his daughter. "You?"

Magda nodded. He hugged her tight. "Child of the May, my Child of the May," he whispered.

⟨21⟩

THE FIRES OF
ALL HALLOWS

THE VILLAGERS WATCHED helplessly as Langden Manor burned. But Isabel did not fret. "We'll build another," she said. "It was damp and cold. Not all our memories are happy ones."

Marian took her arm. "Let's turn this misery to good," she said.

Isabel smiled at her, puzzled.

"Did we not wish for costumes and bonfires?"

"Aye." Isabel began to understand. "We can turn our fire to celebration."

And suddenly she was rushing about, ordering fowls to be slaughtered and food prepared. "Is there grain left for soul cakes?" she asked.

"There certainly is," Margery told her. "I dragged three grain sacks from the kitchen and hid them in my mother's hut. There's honey too. I wasn't going to feed them honey!"

Isabel flung her arms about the girl.

Brother James and Tom came pushing through the crowd to find Robert. "You'll like this!" they told him. They could not stop laughing and slapping each other.

"Whatever can you find so funny?" Philippa asked.

"The sheriff," cried Brother James. "The villagers have

got him bound and gagged in one of their huts. They wish to hang him."

"No!" Philippa chuckled. "Hanging's too good. We should roast him alive!"

As darkness fell, the villagers fetched out trestle tables and stools and set them up around the still-burning ruins of the manor house. They brought trenchers of fresh-baked bread piled high with nuts and fruit and little honey-sweetened soul cakes. Small cooking fires were lit around the main blaze, and children set to turn the spits. Soon Langden was full of delicious smells as roasting fowls were slowly cooked. Jugs of good barley ale were brought from the cottages, and Isabel gathered her friends for a strange feast.

The Knights of Saint Lazarus were given the seats of honor. They accepted politely but remained in their own small group, keeping a distance from the crowd.

Tom, with Alan at his side, went hesitantly toward the quiet, hooded fighting men. Walter of Stainthorpe turned and saw their approach. He held up his hand to stop them.

"Show your clapper," Tom told Alan.

The boy snatched up the clapper that swung at his belt and sent it clacking. There was sudden quiet as all turned to see what was happening. The leper knights looked at one another for a moment, but then Walter of Stainthorpe pulled up a stool and beckoned the boy to sit with them.

Robert sat with Marian, deep in thought, his face mottled in the flickering light and shadows. He was silent despite the celebration all around him.

"What is it?" Marian took his hand. "Why are you so miserable, when we are celebrating? Never have outlaws been so welcome at a feast. You saved us!"

"Aye, but for how long, sweetheart?" he asked.

Marian frowned too then, and sighed. She could see that he was right. How long would it be before the sheriff's men came hunting them, their numbers swelled and weapons sharp?

"But just a moment!" said Robert. "I think I have an idea." A slow smile touched the corner of his mouth.

"What now?" Marian demanded.

Robert burst out laughing. "I have it!" he said. "John, bring the sheriff here!"

John looked a little surprised but did as his friend asked and dragged the terrified man from the hut toward the fire.

"Aye," said Philippa. "I said we should roast him!"

The sheriff buckled at the knees with fright, and Philippa burst out laughing.

"Untie his hands!" said Robert. There were gasps of surprise from all around, but Tom quickly cut the sheriff's bonds.

"Where's Magda?" Robert cried. "Come here, Magda! Do you remember our feast in Nottingham Castle?"

"Aye."

"Now we shall return the compliment. The sheriff's lady made us guests and showed us a little kindness too."

"Yes," Isabel agreed. "The sheriff's lady let me bring my mother safe home."

Robert picked up a stool and courteously invited the sheriff to sit and eat. The man was white-faced and petrified, but sat as he was bidden. Quiet fell as the villagers stared. Then resentful muttering rose all around.

"Has the Hooded One gone mad?"

"Drunk?"

"Stupid?"

But Marian put fresh roast meat onto a trencher and

passed it to the sheriff. "It's plain but wholesome," she told him. "Eat up!"

Warily the sheriff began to nibble at his food.

"When we have feasted," Robert bellowed, "we will see our sheriff dance around our bonfire."

There was laughter then and protests faded. Soon everyone was eating and drinking again.

It was noon the next day when they all woke. They'd slept late on the floors of Langden's huts; now they yawned and stretched and wearily prepared to return to their homes.

But before they went, Isabel gathered visitors and villagers alike around the still-smoking mound of the manor house. Lady Matilda was carried out on a litter and gently lowered to the ground. Then John led forward the sheriff and his horse. The man was pale, clearly still fearful that they'd kill him.

Once more Robert ordered the man's hands untied. Brother James and Mother Veronica unrolled two carefully written sheets of parchment that they'd been working on. Brother James read them out loud so that all the assembled villagers could hear.

" 'I, Gilbert de Gore, High Sheriff of Nottinghamshire, Yorkshire, and Derbyshire, do solemnly declare that the Lady Matilda of Langden shall dispose of her daughter, Isabel, in marriage where she will. This I assert in the name of His Majesty King John, whom as Shire Reeve I represent. To be witnessed by Veronica, Prioress of Saint Mary Magdalen's nuns, and Sir Walter of Stainthorpe, Knight of the Order of Saint Lazarus.' "

A ripple of surprise and agreement went around the gathering as at last the villagers began to see some sense in

Robert's madness. The sheriff was given pen and ink, and he glumly signed both papers.

"Now," cried Robert, "fasten him to his horse."

The sheriff's face was red with shame as he was roughly tied onto his horse, wrong way round. Robert rolled up one of the parchments and thrust it into the sheriff's jerkin.

Walter of Stainthorpe took up the other, handling it carefully in his gloved gauntlets. "This copy shall be kept in the preceptory of Bitterwood," he said. "Should the agreement be broken, I shall call upon my Templar brethren to bring about the execution of justice."

The sheriff nodded, sick at the very thought. Robert bent forward and spoke low to him. "Thank your lady wife for your life!" he hissed.

Then he slapped the horse's backside, and Tom led the miserable man away from Langden toward the bounds of Clipstone.

Later that day the Knights of Saint Lazarus saddled their horses and packed the armor and weapons that had provided disguise. Walter of Stainthorpe strode close to where Alan stood with Tom.

"Boy?" he called in his husky voice. "We have need of one strong fellow to come with us and help us with our steeds and gear."

"Me?" cried Alan, his face lighting up.

"Who better?" Walter asked.

Alan took a step forward eagerly. "I'll come, sir, willingly; but might I not stay with you? I'd serve you, sir, in any way I could."

"Aye? Indeed!" Walter cried. "Would you learn to be my squire?"

Doubt and delight showed clear on Alan's face. "You'll have me?"

"Certainly! You shall be my squire, and if you train hard to fight and pray, maybe in time you shall be knight!"

Then as Alan went with Tom to collect his few belongings, Walter of Stainthorpe went down on one knee before Mother Veronica. He took her hand in his great gauntlet. "Madam, I am still your knight," he said.

When at last it was time for them to go, Magda went to Alan hesitantly. She took his hand and pressed it to her face. Tears spilled down her cheeks.

"Don't cry," he whispered. "I am happier than I ever thought to be. Someday I'll come back and spar with you."

EPILOGUE

THE FORESTWIFE and her friends gathered at Langden for the Christmas feasts. The sturdy new manor house had been built with great effort before the coldest weather came. New Langden Manor was smaller and cozier, and Matilda and Isabel insisted that Christmas there was better than ever, with their friends all gathered about them.

There was sudden anxiety when, in the middle of the meal, a red-faced kitchen lad announced the arrival of men and horses in the sheriff's livery. Everyone got up from the table fearfully and ran to the door. Worries were soon turned to delight. It was not an armed guard, but a packhorse train, loaded with warm rugs and fine worked wall hangings: presents to Lady Matilda from the sheriff's wife.

Winter passed, and Langden and Barnsdale knew peace. The simple Christmas gifts had done much to calm nagging doubts, and as spring returned the forest folk planned their May Day revels once more.

It was May Day morning, and inside the Forestwife's cottage the fire was crackling.

"Hold still!" Marian cried.

Magda found it hard not to wriggle as Marian fastened the laces on the fine white linen gown that Isabel had brought for her. This year Marian had insisted right from the start that she was far too ancient to be the Green Lady.

The old one nodded mysteriously. "It should be Magda," she said. "Best she learns soon what she must do."

Magda frowned. "What do you mean? Can you see what my life will be?"

Eleanor shook her head. "I cannot see it all, sweetheart, but this I know: that fine worked girdle round Marian's waist shall one day be yours."

Magda caught her breath. "I will be Forestwife?" Suddenly loving and fearful, she went and put her arms around Marian's neck.

Eleanor smiled. "Not for a long time yet, but someday."

"But if Robert is old or gone, there'll be no Hooded One to help me."

Marian and Eleanor both laughed, and Eleanor spoke firmly. "There will always be a Forestwife, and there will always be a Hooded One."

In the distance they heard faint voices singing sweetly, but Magda was not satisfied. "Who will he be?" she insisted.

Eleanor shook her head. "Look to the Green Man," she said.

"I thought that would be Father or Robert."

Magda was uncertain about dancing with the Green Man if she didn't know who it was hidden inside all those leaves, but there was no time left to worry. The singers were at the door, demanding to crown her.

Marian kissed her. "Don't be afraid," she said. "You will enjoy being May Queen."

Eleanor flung the door open, and the hut was filled with children. They crowned Magda with sweet-smelling hawthorn and dragged her out to the maypole by the trysting tree. Robert and John were waiting there for them. Marian went to hug them both, while the children ran off into the woods.

"Who can he be?" Magda whispered, her heart thumping wildly.

At last the children were returning, dragging the strange leaf-clad figure out from the shadows into the sunlight.

Magda bit her lip and twisted her fingers together. The Green Man came dancing toward her . . . then suddenly she caught her breath and smiled with understanding. The Green Man was tall and beautiful, but as he danced and twirled, he dragged his right leg just a little. Magda held out her arms and ran toward him—the magical Green Man.